J.T. EDSON'S
FLOATING OUTFIT

The toughest bunch of Rebels that ever lost a war, they fought for the South, and then for Texas, as the legendary Floating Outfit of "Ole Devil" Hardin's O.D. Connected ranch.

MARK COUNTER was the best-dressed man in the West: always dressed fit-to-kill. BELLE BOYD was as deadly as she was beautiful, with a "Manhattan" model Colt tucked under her long skirts. THE YSABEL KID was Comanche fast and Texas tough. And the most famous of them all was DUSTY FOG, the ex-cavalryman known as the Rio Hondo Gun Wizard.

J. T. Edson has captured all the excitement and adventure of the raw frontier in this magnificent Western series. Turn the page for a complete list of Berkley Floating Outfit titles.

J. T. EDSON'S
FLOATING OUTFIT
WESTERN ADVENTURES
FROM BERKLEY

J.T. Edson

GUNS IN THE NIGHT

BERKLEY BOOKS, NEW YORK

GUNS IN THE NIGHT

A Berkley Book/published by arrangement with
Transworld Publishers, Ltd.

PRINTING HISTORY
Corgi edition published 1968
Berkley edition/July 1985

ISBN: 0-425-07972-4

A BERKLEY BOOK® TM 757,375
Berkley Books are published by The Berkley Publishing Group,
200 Madison Avenue, New York, New York 10016.
The name "BERKLEY" and the stylized "B"
with design are trademarks belonging to
Berkley Publishing Corporation.
PRINTED IN THE UNITED STATES OF AMERICA

CHAPTER ONE

Thunder in the Night

Down to the south, in the far distance, thunder rolled and a flicker of lightning ripped the storm-laden heavens, creasing the sky momentarily then fading into nothing. None of the trio of riders heading south from Kansas showed the slightest sign of concern at the sight, although they were far from human shelter, for they knew the storm would not come their way.

"Ole *Ka-Dih's* riled tonight," said the Ysabel Kid as his wild-looking, seventeen-hand-high white stallion eased itself with cat-footed grace down a cut-bank's slope.

"Damned if at times you don't believe in that Comanche Great Spirit, Lon," answered Mark Counter, sitting his huge bloodbay stud casually, a light rider despite his giant size. "What do you reckon, Dusty?"

Dusty Fog smiled. *"Ka-Dih,* Great Spirit, God. It's all one and the same. A man needs something to believe in. Especially on a stormy night."

And with that Dusty gave the pack-horse's hackamore a gentle twitch as a reminder to stay close to his big, magnificent paint stallion's flank while they crossed the cutback.

"We won't make the Starr place tonight, that's for sure," drawled the Kid. "Not without riding through that storm. Which same, I hate water except for drinking and washing in; and if I wash, I don't want to do it dressed."

"We'll bed down soon as we can then," Mark replied.

One might have expected Dusty Fog to make such a

1

decision, being the other two's employer. However, the matter on hand was Mark Counter's concern and Dusty willingly allowed his good amigo full say in whether they halted or pushed on down to the Starr ranch through the night and the storm.

"There's a spring about half a mile on," remarked the Kid, his part-Indian ability to follow a path, or remember a strip of land in darkness or daylight, locating their position on the Oklahoma range. "Be the best place to bed down. What do you reckon Belle wants with you, Mark?"

"Sounded real urgent," Dusty agreed.

"She just said for us to get down here as quickly as we could," Mark replied, his voice a deep, cultured Southern drawl.

"Could be she wants to marry up with you at last. Mark boy," grinned the Kid. "Only I don't reckon you'd be riding *towards* her if you thought that."

"Wouldn't I?" asked Mark.

Something in the way his big *amigo* spoke brought Dusty's eyes jerking in Mark's direction. A man did not share food, fun, danger and work with another for ten years without getting to know how the other thought, felt and acted; so Dusty noticed Mark's tone more than would a stranger. During their quartet of days in Mulrooney at the end of a cattle drive, Mark had been somewhat quiet and subdued, although again, only a good friend would have noticed it. Dusty had been inclined to put Mark's behavior down to the knowledge that this would most likely be the last of the great inter-state drives. The way railroads were being driven south into Texas, next year a man would not need to make the long drive north to the Kansas trail-end. As a working cattleman and the segundo of the biggest ranch in Texas, Dusty approved of the change, but also regretted it a little too. Driving a herd of around three thousand head of half-wild longhorn Texas cattle through the danger, against inclement elements, in the face of a hundred and more problems, without losing many head, had been an achievement. After the long days on the trail, the arrival of the shipping pens had been greeted with such joy that only a man who experienced it could understand. It was a time for fun, wild horse-play, reckless spending of hard-earned money, drinking and love-making—or what passed for love-making in most cases.

On previous drives Mark could always be found in the thick of the fun and frolics, ready to dance all night, get involved in a fight or make even the most blasé dance-hall girl's pulse beat the quicker with his adroit love-making. Not so on their last trip. Mark showed, if only to Dusty, a remarkable lack of interest in the high times offered by Mulrooney. However, Dusty had for once been too busy with his own affairs to wonder at Mark's unusual lassitude and preoccupation. Freddie Woods, lady mayor of Mulrooney, leading citizen and saloon-keeper, and Dusty were old friends, in fact on his previous visit had become really close.* After the first day, by tradition given over to helping his trail drive crew to whoop up a storm celebration, Dusty spent most of his time with Freddie and so did not become fully aware of Mark's changed attitude until the third day. Things had progressed far with Freddie during that time and might have gone much further had Mark not received a request from Belle Starr to visit her as soon as possible.

That the famous lady outlaw should contact Mark in no way surprised the blond giant or his friends. Belle and Mark's path had crossed more than once; the last time some three months before when Mark came across her while handling a lone chore for his boss, Ole Devil Hardin. Just what

*Told in *The Fortune Hunters*, by J. T. Edson.

happened on that meeting only Mark and Belle knew, but Dusty noticed a growing change in his friend and wondered at it.

Knowing how things stood between Dusty and Freddie, Mark hesitated before asking his two friends to ride with him. However, Freddie was shrewd as well as very beautiful and read the problem. Coming from a stock which never hesitated to accept its responsibilities—she was, in fact, a titled English lady whose yen to travel brought her out West and love of adventure established her as joint owner of the biggest and best saloon in Mulrooney—Freddie did not hesitate. She and Dusty discussed the matter and another very serious subject, one which might affect their whole lives. Calmly, without histrionics or emotions showing, Freddie stated that Dusty must ride with Mark as they had ridden into danger so many times before. At the conclusion of what ever trouble lay ahead of them, Dusty could make his decision.

"If you want me, Dusty," she told him, "send word and I'll come."

Dusty knew full well what Freddie meant. With the trail drives in the process of coming to an end there would be little to bring Dusty north to Kansas and Mulrooney's golden heyday had ended. Having proved herself capable of making a financial and actual success, Freddie was now willing to fulfill her destiny as a woman. Riding south with Mark and the Kid, Dusty thought long on the matter, wondering if he could marry and settle down. Yet so many of the old wild bunch with whom he spent so many happy times had slipped gracefully and uncomplaining into the bonds of matrimony over the last few years and all appeared to be highly satisfied with their lot. It would be marriage if he sent for Freddie, neither she nor he would accept less.

And now, as he listened to Mark's two-word response to the Kid's comment, Dusty wondered if the blond giant was going the same way as Red Blaze, Johnny Raybold, Stone Hart, Doc Leroy and even young Waco. Stranger things had happened on the great cattle range which spread unfenced and free from the Mississippi to the Pacific shore. Belle Starr was a beautiful, intelligent young woman and had never gone so far beyond the law's fringe that she could not chance settling down into matrimony. Once in a while Belle had descended into bloodless hold-ups, but only if the reward be high enough and the chance of endangering lives all but non-existent; she specialized in carefully thought-out and planned swindles, choosing her victims with care and leaving them poorer but never destitute. If Belle decided to settle down, and Mark agreed, Dusty reckoned they would make an ideal man and wife.

Knowing Mark as well as did Dusty, the Ysabel Kid also noticed the blond giant's tone. From the look of things, the Kid figured he might be seeing his two best friends, men closer to him than any brothers, slide away into married life. A slow grin creased his face, yet in his heart the Kid felt a little sad. Life would be very dull without Dusty and Mark's presence—for the Kid knew marriage and riding as a member of a trouble-shooting floating outfit did not mix.

Ahead of them, water glinted dully in the darkness. The spring welled up into a small lake, trickled off in a stream which disappeared into a large clump of scrub-oak and pin-ion trees. Ignoring the storm which still raged far to the south, the three friends swung from their saddles and pre-pared to settle down for the night. Leaving the other two to tend to their saddle horses and the pack animals, the Kid faded off into the clump of trees, a *bosque* as it would have been called in Texas and the South-West territories. With an almost cat-like ability to see in the dark, the Kid gathered dried wood and soon returned to the spring with enough to light a fire.

Once, Oklahoma Territory, the Indian Nations as it was

known, had been a real dangerous area. The tribes of Indians, herded to Oklahoma as being an area the white brother did not require for his expansion, might be held on reservations, but always some bad-hat buck would be ready to slip away from his appointed dwelling place, gather a few good friends and fall back to the ways of the good old days when taking the white-eyed brother's scalp had been a pleasant pastime. Old habits die hard, and remembering the good old days on the Indian Nations, the Kid did not build too large a fire. He and his friends had long been used to hardship and spending a night with the sky for a roof and the earth as a mattress held no terrors for them—although the comfort-loving Mark never settled to such a night's rest without bitter complaint.

Working fast, the Ysabel Kid lit his fire and its flames illuminated the three young men, each of whom was a legend within his own lifetime.

Standing by the fire, laying down his low-horned, double-girthed—no Texan used the word cinch—range saddle, Mark Counter towered above the other two. The firelight played on his curly, golden blond hair and almost classically handsome face, a face that showed intelligence and strength of will. Great spreading shoulders hinted at the enormous biceps under the costly made-to-measure tan shirt's sleeves and spoke of the strength which gave Mark the name of being a rangeland Hercules. From there he slimmed down to a lean fighting man's waist, strong hips and long powerful legs which stood him full six foot three inches over the ground. An expensive white Stetson hat, low of crown, wide brimmed in the Texas style and with silver concha decorated band around it, sat on the back of his head. His brown Levis pants were tailored to his fit, for Mark could not buy his size of clothing off a general store's peg, hung cowhand style, cuffs turned back and outside his high-heeled fancy-stitched boots. Around his waist hung a gunbelt made by the dean of Texas leatherworkers, Joe Gaylin, whose master hand also built the boots, and in the holsters, contoured and set just right for a real fast draw, rested matched Colt Cavalry Peacemakers that sported ivory butts and the finest blue Best Citizen's Finish offered by the Hartford factory, yet were still functional fighting weapons.

All in all Mark looked, and was, a range country fashion plate. His taste in clothing dictated what the well-dressed Texan cattle worker wore, just as in the War Between the States his style of uniform had been much copied among the bloods of the Confederate Army. Yet there was more than a dandy dresser about Mark. Possibly he was the finest working cowhand in Texas, knowing every facet of the cattle business. His strength had become a legend, his skill in a rough-house brawl spoken of with bated breath wherever seen. However, few people knew just how fast and good with a gun Mark could be, for he lived in the shadow of the greatest gun fighting exponent of them all. Yet the few who *knew*, claimed Mark to be second only to his good *amigo*, the Rio Hondo gun wizard Dusty Fog. While Mark, having been left a large sum of money in an aunt's will, could have owned his own spread, he preferred instead to ride as a member of the OD Connected ranch crew, working as part of its boss, Ole Devil Hardin's floating outfit.

Drawing the magnificent "One of a Thousand" Winchester Model of 1873 rifle from its saddleboot, the Kid laid it handy by the fire. In the flames his Indian-dark, almost babyishly innocent, handsome face seemed no more than sixteen years of age. Even the red hazel eyes, which hinted of the restless, wild spirit behind the features, seemed relaxed and softened by the fiery glow. All black was the Kid, from the Stetson hat which perched on his curly, raven black hair, through bandana, shirt and levis down to his boots. Around his waist hung a black leather gunbelt and only the ivory grips of the James Black bowie knife at his left side and the brown walnut handle of the old Second Model Colt Dragoon riding butt forward at the right relieved the somber tones of his dress.

Down on the Rio Grande folks still remembered the Ysabel kid and spoke his name in whispers. He had been a wild, reckless youngster in those days, with one foot on the downward slide which led to a picture on a post office wall the word 'WANTED' over it. Then he met Dusty Fog and threw in his lot with the Rio Hondo gun wizard.* From that day the Kid developed into a real useful member of the range country society. Not so much a cowhand as his friends, his true talents lay in the business of riding scout: there the Kid claimed few peers and no betters. Son of a wild Irish-Kentuckian fighting man and a French Creole-Comanche girl, the Kid grew up with all the best qualities of those fighting breeds. Keen of eye and ear, capable of silent movement through the thickest cover, able to read tracks with the ease of a buck Apache, with the inborn ability to carry the map of area in his head or find his way across the open range, the Kid had many uses to offer in his chosen field. While he could not honestly claim to be fast with a gun—it took him all of a second to draw and shoot, and a fast man almost halved that time—the Kid acknowledged no master in the art of handling a bowie knife, nor did he know any more accomplished maestro in the use of the Winchester rifle. The magnificent gun by the fire came to him as first prize at the Cochise Country Fair, when he matched his skill against some of the finest shots in the West.† Taken all into consideration, the Ysabel Kid was a

---

*Told in *The Ysabel Kid*, by J. T. Edson.
†Told in *Gun Wizard*, by J. T. Edson.

young man it paid well to keep as a friend, for he made a real bad enemy.

The firelight also played its witch glow upon Dusty Fog; the man said to be the fastest and most accurate of all the gunfighting breed; who rode as captain commanding his own troops of Confederate cavalry when but seventeen years old, and made a name to equal that of Turner Ashby or John Singleton Mosby as a military raider of the finest type. With the War over, Dusty Fog had not slipped into a morass of self-pity, or brooded about the glorious future that would surely have been his if the Confederate States won. Instead he set to work, helping his uncle Ole Devil Hardin rebuild the great OD Connected ranch. Now Dusty Fog was known as the segundo, second-in-command of the ranch; a cattle-man of the first-water; a trail boss in the great tradition of Oliver Loving and Charles Goodnight. Men also spoke of how his guns, cool courage, hard fists and shrewd knowl-edge of human nature tamed two bad wild towns when lesser men died trying.

What kind of a man could he then be, this giant among his fellows.

Dusty Fog stood but five foot five and a half inches in height. Yet he was far from being puny. If Dusty had been as tall as Mark, he would have shown at least as good a muscular development, but his physique did not display itself except in a moment of need. While handsome, Dusty did not have the eye-catching quality of his two good friends. Nor, though they cost as much, did his clothes look so fine as those of either Mark or the Kid. A Texas-style black Stetson hat sat Dusty's dusty blond hair, a tight rolled silk bandana trailed long ends over his blue shirt. Cowhand style Levis hung outside expensive Gaylin boots. Good clothing all, yet Dusty managed to make them look like they came off the peg of a poorer-class general store. Around his waist hung a Gaylin gunbelt, its contoured holsters bearing a brace of matched, bone-handled Colt Civilian Peacemakers, the butts turned forward for a cross-hand draw. Even that finest example of leatherwork did little to make its wearer more noticeable—until Dusty Fog needed the guns for some purpose.

Long practice at setting up a temporary camp for the night showed in the way the three friends went about their work. Without discussing the matter, each of the trio knew his duty and started working on it. Taking the coffeepot, Dusty walked to the edge of the water. A movement further along brought him turning his left hand flickering out and thumb-cocking the right-side Colt. Hooves drummed rapidly as some animal appeared from the bushes by the edge of the stream. Too small for a longhorn lost from a passing herd, Dusty noticed with relief; for a longhorn feared human beings only when they sat afork a horse, and would charge a man on foot at sight. The animal had neither the bulk of a Plains bison—few of which remained in the meat-hungry Indian Nations—nor the magnificent antler-spread of a wapiti, or elk as most folks called it; both of which could show truculence when come upon suddenly at night and on foot. Too small for a Kansas whitetail deer, certainly not a grizzly or black bear, or a cougar. Then the animal whirled and fled, a white splash showed briefly as the animal burned the breeze, not for the trees but out across the open range. From that flicker of white, and the speed at which the animal departed, Dusty knew it to be a pronghorn antelope, an old buck driven from his herd by a younger more virile male. Grinning a little, Dusty holstered his Colt and collected the water.

Back at the camp, Mark took hobbles from the pack and shackled the horse they used to carry their bedrolls, saving weight on their personal mounts and allowing them to make better time. With the horse fixed so that it could move around and graze, but not stray far or escape in the morning when needed to resume its duties, Mark removed the pack and carried it to the fire where he and the Kid unfastened the tarpaulin cover to get at what they needed for the night. Both heard the rush of hooves and Mark's right hand dipped, sliding the seven and a half inch barrelled Colt from the offside holster fast. However, the Kid just threw one quick glance in the direction of the sound and gave a grinning grunt.

"Pronghorn," he said. "You're sure jumpy tonight, *amigo.*"

"Reckon I am," agreed Mark, sliding the Colt back to leather.

"What'd you do," asked the Kid as Dusty returned carrying the coffeepot, "walk all over the poor fool critter as it slept?"

"What poor fool critter?" inquired Dusty innocently, setting the pot on the flames.

"That pronghorn that just went by here like a devil after a yearling."

"Was there a pronghorn?" countered Dusty, his very innocence of tone telling his friend that he had been startled by the animal and most likely made the natural reaction to such a situation.

"Ole Mark here damned nigh blew my head off throwing down on it," answered the Kid. "Never afore rode with two such jumpy cusses. Happen that's what being in love does to a man——"

"Always say that loving and winning a gal's a whole heap more fun than just going up to her pappy and buying her with a bunch of stolen hosses," stated Mark. "Which they do tell is the mean Comanche habit."

"Sure is," agreed the Kid. "Saves a man a whole heap of time and effort."

"Which same reminds me of something Freddie told me

about one of her kin back in England," Dusty put in. "Want to hear it?"

"Nope," answered Mark." "But seeing's how you're our boss, I don't reckon we've any real choice."

"That's what I like," grinned the small Texan. "Loyal hired help."

"Just tell us this here pack of lies so's we can get some sleep," groaned the Kid, but waited eagerly; for Miss Freddie Woods possessed a fund of good stories which suited the Western cowhand's taste in such matters.

"Well, this cousin, he's an earl or something, finally got around to asking Lady something-or-other to marry him. You know the British, all stiff, formal and proper in their ways."

"We know," chuckled Mark, thinking of the rip-roaring feud between the "proper in her ways" Miss Woods and her rival in the saloon business and how the two ladies settled their differences in what must have been a real fine brawl.*

"Well, this cousin got married and about a month later his wife said to him, 'Sir James, I'm afraid we aren't going to have a baby,' and he answered, 'Good Lord! Does that mean we have to go through that revolting business again?'"

Although bubbling with mirth, Mark and the Kid managed to keep their faces straight as they studied Dusty.

"Happen that's how them English folks feel about it," said the Kid. "I'd sure think twice afore I married Freddie."

"She wouldn't have to think twice about *not* marrying you," growled Mark.

"I'd surely hope she wouldn't," answered the Kid. "Couldn't raise me enough hosses to pay for a real lady like Freddie—or Belle."

The banter went on among the three friends, biting, crit-

*Told in *The Trouble Busters*, by J. T. Edson.

ical, yet gentle underneath, until they finished their meal. Then they spread their bedrolls, slid beneath covers and allowing the fire to die down, went to sleep. Before sleep finally came Dusty and Mark did some thinking and their thoughts followed the same lines—should they take the women they loved and settle down as married men?

CHAPTER TWO

Guns in the Night

Suddenly the Ysabel Kid woke up. There was no interim period of sluggish semi-daze, just a swift, silent transition from hard asleep to fully awake and alert awareness of what went on around him. Laying without a movement, his head pillowed on his saddle, the Kid started to figure out what woke him.

Down to the south the storm still raged, but such an everpresent, though distant, noise would not disturb him any more than had the closer restless movement of the four horses. Not far away a Great Horned owl screeched as it flittered on silent wings in search of food, and from the ground came the chatter of a disturbed covey of bob-white quail startled by the prowling hunter. However, such a natural noise, one likely to be heard any night upon the range, would never bring the Kid out of his sleep.

In the *bosque* beyond the camp, a bush rustled and to its right a twig snapped gently. Instantly the Kid tensed in his bedroll and reached for the worn walnut handle of his old Dragoon Colt. No animal ever made so much noise when moving in the darkness. Only man, with his feeble powers of scent, sight, touch and sound scraped against rustling objects, or placed clumsy feet upon breakable, noise-creating twigs. And if men came, attracted by the glowing, dying embers of the fire, they came with evil intent. Travelers with good intentions rode up openly, or if on foot, announced their coming with shouts or other noises. Oklahoma Territory possessed a good quota of outlaws, driven out of better policed areas, and including some of the worst, meanest cusses in the West. To the Kid's way of thinking, the stalkers in the night must be white. Few Indian tribes raided at night and the Kid doubted if any Indian brave-heart would make so much noise when sneaking up to do murder, or counter coup, on the sleeping white-eye brother's camp.

"Dusty! Mark!" he hissed.

Low though the Kid's voice came pitched, Dusty and Mark woke instantly; alert, yet neither speaking, making any noise nor sitting up. To all appearances the camp remained as it had been before the Kid awoke, with one unseen but very important difference. Now all three shapes in the bedrolls were fully awake and ready, their faculties working full time.

"Hear 'em?" asked the Kid in no louder tone than his first two words.

No reply for a few seconds, then Dusty answered, "Just about."

"We're not all danged Comanches," Mark went on. "Four or five up in the trees, I'd say."

"That many for sure," agreed the Kid. "Only that's not all. There's at least three more moved out on each flank and, 'less I miss my guess, another one coming all quiet and sneaky down towards the hosses."

"Poor bastard," answered Mark dryly, for he knew the nature of the Kid's huge white stallion.

"Reckon we'd best get set to greet 'em formally," Dusty suggested.

Although they had not expected the storm to swing in their direction, the three Texans had prepared their beds for the chance of catching some of its side fringe of rain. Making their sleeping arrangements for the night, each of the trio spread his blankets and suggans upon the seven by eighteen feet sheet of white No. 8 ducking used to wrap around and give its waterproof protection to the bedding and war bag during the day. Folding the edge of the ducking over and coupling the hook and eye fasteners in place, each man slid into the waiting bed, using their saddles, or in Mark's case a small, soft pillow, to rest their heads. Should the rain come, drawing up the flap of the ducking would form a cover over the head and the sleeper could lie safe from the elements in a warm bed.

Unfortunately the clipped edges of the ducking did not make for speedy rising and so each man cautiously and silently reached out his hands to unfasten the hooks, then gently eased open the blankets. With that done, and free, easy and rapid egress from the bed ensured, the trio gave thought to the armament they would need in the near future. Such a decision gave Dusty and Mark little trouble and each drew his rightside weapon ready for use. Knowing his limitations in the handling of a revolver, the Kid preferred to place his firearms emphasis on the extra range and superior magazine capacity of the Winchester. However, from his considerable knowledge of night fighting, he realized he might need something easier to handle at close range than the rifle would be. Leaving the rifle, he drew his old Dragoon from leather, its four pound two ounce weight nothing considering its thumb-busting power. Almost instinctively the Kid's left hand slid out his bowie knife, for he never felt entirely happy relying solely upon a handgun in a fight.

Armed and ready, the three Texans lay silent, watchful, just waiting for the first clear indication of their enemies' position. By now the embers of the fire had died down to such a point that the camp lay in darkness as much as did the surrounding range.

The member of the stalking party who had circled the

camp now moved forward on his belly, sliding through the foot-high grass like a snake, a single shot Springfield cavalry carbine resting on his hands. All his party carried such weapons, so wished to get in as close as possible to the sleeping camp before starting to shoot. A Springfield carbine had but one quality to command it, low production cost— a prime deciding factor in times of peace when Congress objected to spending on the Army money that could be used for vote-gathering projects. So the cavalry, and the current raiding party, found themselves armed with a gun sadly lacking in power and accuracy, a very pig to reload, due to inexplicable jamming of its works. Not a weapon upon which a man cared to take long chances when his life stood as one of the stakes in the game. Not knowing what kind of men lay sleeping in the camp, but being fully aware that skill with arms was the rule not the exception among travelers in the Indian Nations, the raiding party had decided to surround the camp, then glide in close and attack from a range where one shot apiece ought to settle the matter.

When laying their plan of campaign, it fell upon this man to circle the sleeping camp and secure as many of the victim's horses as possible. Not that he objected to the order. Let the others take on the more risky tasks of encircling the camp and jumping its occupants, he would handle his end of the affair and grab the pick of the captured horses for himself.

With eyes grown used to piercing the darkness, the man spotted shapes and identified them as being horses. One, two, three—no, a fourth grazed a little way from the others. That meant at least four men by the fire. If the quartet carried the normal armaments of rifle and revolver, most of the raiding party would soon possess a more effective weapon than a single-shot carbine.

Crawling nearer, the man studied the horses as well as

he could. One of the animals turned his way, letting out a low snort on detecting a shape sliding through the grass towards it. The man thought little about this warning sound, other than to notice the animal appeared to be an exceptional fine-looking, light-coloured creature.

Suddenly the horse gave another snort, and charged straight at the crawling man, a stallion's shrill fighting scream ringing out. Still not unduly worried, the man reared up to his knees, figuring that showing the horse that he was a human being would stop its rush. A sudden shock of apprehension and fear hit the man as he saw that the horse did not stop. On it came, rearing high into the air with steel-shod hooves churning out savagely. Too late the man tried to swing his carbine into line. One of the hooves drove down, smashing into the man's head. Involuntarily a finger closed on the carbine's trigger and a shot roared out. Neither the sound of the shot nor the searing blaze of the muzzle-blast scared off the horse, and the bullet flew into the night harmlessly. The man pitched forward and the horse, still screaming in rage, lashed down on the still shape. At first the impact of the hooves sounded crisp and hard, then changed to dull, soggy thuds interspersed with cracks as bones splintered under the stamping kicks.

The unexpected attack of the Kid's stallion threw a fairly good plan for looting and murder out of kilter. Hideous though the sounds were, they affected the three Texans, who knew the horse's ways and expected something of the kind, less than the attackers. Startled yells rang out around the camp, bringing an angry, disbelieving growl from the Kid. Then guns thundered in the darkness and lead came screaming down towards the area of the fire.

Taken all in all, the attackers shot with fair accuracy. Dusty's bedroll jerked as a bullet lashed into it, but the small Texan no longer lay inside. The moment he heard the

noise of the horse's attack, Dusty knew he must get clear
of the bedroll—and fast. Colt in his left hand, he thrust
himself from the blankets and hugged the ground as he went.
Even as Dusty moved, his two friends also vacated their
bedrolls and prepared to make war. Without needing dis-
cussion or orders, each of the trio knew what his two amigos
would do, how they could be expected to react to the situation, and so planned his own move accordingly. Dusty
wound up facing the left side, and closest, bunch, counting
three shots in his direction. Rolling clear of his bed, Mark
brought out his second Colt in passing and wound up facing
towards the three men who, some thirty yards away, threw
shots towards the camp. Knowing the white could handle
its side, the Kid remained free to concentrate his efforts on
the rest of the attackers, four at least, who used their guns
from the edge of the *bosque,* a good fifty yards from the
Texans' bed ground.

Skilled in the art of night fighting, Dusty held his fire
until the other side tipped their hands by throwing lead and
so showing their positions. The men appeared to be bunched
close together in a manner which showed a remarkable
faith—or considerable lack of foresight. Dusty threw three
fast shots, fanning them in an arc towards where the flickering muzzle-blasts showed his mark. From the way one of
the dark shapes jerked, stumbled and fell, he guessed that
some of the lead connected. Although Dusty did not know
it, a second attacker felt the wind of a bullet by his face,
mute testimony to the small Texan's skill with a gun under
difficult conditions.

On firing, Dusty rolled over and over until clear of the
place from which he threw lead. No answering shots came
to his ears but, despite the bellowing of Mark's guns, he
heard a dull clicking noise which he recognized as the
operation noise of a Springfield's trap-door breech.

"Singleshot army guns!" Dusty mused and pondered a little on what such a sound once meant in the Indian Nations.

Flame licked out and a gun bellowed. Dusty heard lead strike to his right and guessed the bullet struck on the spot from which he fired. Two more bullets lanced from his gun and he rolled back to the left. Clearly the second man had been waiting for Dusty to shoot, for another carbine spat and flying dirt struck the small Texan's shirt as it erupted under the impact of a close-landing bullet. Taking a chance that the third man was out of the game, Dusty used his last bullet and heard a muffled yelp of pain.

While Dusty could, and often had, reloaded his Colt in the darkness, he did not take the time. A swift wriggle carried him to his bedroll where he exchanged the Colt for his Winchester '73 carbine. Behind him the shooting had stopped and he wondered how his two friends had fared.

Mark followed Dusty's tactics in leaving his bedroll, getting clear and allowing the enemy to make the first move. However, at a range of thirty yards, more than double the distance from which the men fired at Dusty, using a Colt one-handed would be unlikely to prove successful. Laying aside his lefthand gun, Mark planted his elbows upon the ground and supported his other Colt with both hands, taking careful sight at where the flame of burning powder had pinpointed his assailants. A skilled fighting man, he had automatically counted the shots coming his way. Only two, and now he heard the sound of reloading a Springfield carbine.

Aiming by memory and at the sound of one of the Springfields, Mark fired. Immediately he rolled over and it was well for him that he did. Off to the left of the two attackers came lead from yet a third man. Apparently that jasper ignored the noise of the stallion's attack on his comrade, or maybe he had been so shocked at the noise that he could

not squeeze a trigger. If the latter, he appeared to be over
his shock now, for his bullet stirred the material of Mark's
shirt in passing and ended its flight harmlessly among the
embers of the fire.

Landing on his stomach, Mark reared into a shooting
position, sighted and fired at the third attacker. A scream
of agony rang out, being echoed by the two cracks as the
first two attackers cut loose again. However, they must have
fired without taking too careful aim, for neither bullet came
near enough to worry Mark. Knowing the men now had
empty carbines, and figuring the third attacker to be out of
the game, Mark thumbed off the remaining loads of his Colt
towards the pair of gun flashes. From the sound of departing
foot-steps, Mark concluded the pair had taken enough. He
wondered why the attackers contented themselves in using
those Springfield carbines. No man would do so if he wore
a Colt at his side. Most white men owned a revolver of
some kind, even if their finances did not run to supplying
fodder for a repeating rifle. Few Indians ever carried a side
arm, or at least not a handgun, preferring to do their work
with a rifle or carbine and handle the close-up business with
knife or war axe. Yet the Indians of the Oklahoma Territory
had been quiet for the past year or more—which they even
had a real fancy school for the young bucks; if rumor be
true, many of the Indian young men who might have taken
the war path now attended school instead. Of course, there
would always be bad Indians, just as there would always
be bad white men. Yet somehow the attack did not strike
Mark as being of Indian efficiency. Give him his due, the
red brave-heart could be relied on to do much better than
this attack when setting out to count coup on the white-eye
brother.

After the volley of shots ripped from among the bushes
that fringed the *bosque*, the Ysabel Kid came up and darted

forward in a silent, crouching, swerving run. He counted five spurts of flame ahead of him, but the Lord only knew where the bullets went. None came near enough to the Kid for him to hear the vicious "Whap!" as one passed close by. Much the same thoughts churned through the Kid's head as assailed Dusty and Mark. The whole attack smacked of Indian work, yet did not have that added touch of brilliance which marked the finest redman's efforts.

However, the Kid spent little time in thought, being more concerned in keeping all his faculties working at top pitch so as to locate his enemies before they saw him. Not classing himself as a *pistolero,* an expert with a handgun, the Kid knew he could do nothing at a range of fifty yards, so figured to get in where his limited ability could do as much damage to the enemy while receiving as little injury as possible to himself. A lesser man might have spent time idly cursing his folly at leaving the rifle behind—but a lesser man would never have moved through the darkness to seek out and attack so superior numbered an enemy.

On moved the Kid, silent and alert. Yet, keen though his senses were, he reached the edge of the bushes without locating for certain any of the attackers. On his way forward, he heard the sound of reloading Springfields, but at that distance could not tell from whence the noises came. If he could once get among the attackers, he figured to serve up some consternation and despondency.

A low, muffled exclamation came from the Kid's right; too low for him to catch the words, or even tell what language was used. Swivelling around fast, he saw something ridged over the bushes, and made the shape as that of a Stetson hat. There was no time to think, or to take aim. The Kid cut loose with his Dragoon from hip high, lining instinctively. As if jerked on a string the Stetson bounced into the air, torn off by the Kid's bullet. From the way the dull shape beneath the hat pitched over backwards into the bushes, the Kid figured his lead went up through the man's head to remove the hat. Triggered off by muscular reaction, the dead man's Springfield boomed loud, but its bullet went nowhere near the Kid.

Instantly the Kid followed his man down, springing forward and crouching over the twitching body. Once realizing he would have to shoot, the Kid closed both eyes when the hammer fell. So the muzzle-blast had not temporarily blinded him and he could see plainly what was happening. Ignoring the kicking of the body, the Kid crouched in cover, his black clothing and dark tanned skin merging into the shadows as effectively as if he wore a cloak of invisibility. Excited voices rose around him. English-speaking voices, deep, guttural and with an accent he knew well.

A shape loomed into sight suddenly at the Kid's left, pausing and staring down. If those accents meant what the Kid knew they did, that *hombre* would smell the burnt powder stench that clung around the old Dragoon. The Kid could smell it and figured the other ought to be at least as keen-nosed. Sure enough, the man had come to a halt, crouching slightly and the Kid could hear him sniffing the air like a bluetick hound hitting cougar line. Then a low snarl left the man's lips and he started to swing his carbine. Even in the darkness the Kid caught a glint of metal studs on the gun's woodwork.

No time to swing around and handle the matter with the Dragoon! The thought screamed warningly in the Kid's head and his brain came up like lightning with an answer. At such a moment, the one who reacted swiftest lived—and so it proved. Across lashed the Kid's great bowie knife, headed for the other man. The Kid was still crouching and knew he could not strike the belly hard enough to end the matter in his favor. No matter, he knew another spot almost as good under the circumstances. Coming across low, the razor edge of the eleven and a half inch long blade bit through the man's trouser leg, sinking into the soft flesh of the inside of the thigh and severing both the great saphenous vein and the femoral artery. Blood spurted out on to the Kid's hand as he withdrew the knife, and a scream of agony burst from the stricken man. Letting his carbine fall unheeded, the man stumbled back with hands clawing at the terrible wound in a vain attempt to prevent his life blood spurting out.

Mingled among the screams came the harsh crackle of something forcing through the bushes on the Kid's right side. He whirled, throwing himself backwards and clear of the stricken man as a large shape loomed up. The bark of a Springfield almost deafened the Kid and its muzzle-blast's flame momentarily blinded him, while the heat of the burning powder scorched his cheek and he heard the screech of a *very* close passing bullet, followed by the soggy, dull impact of lead striking human flesh. At the same moment, even as he fell to the ground, the Kid fired and his old Dragoon's deep bellow echoed through the night. He fired by instinct and hoped for the best, trusting that *Ka-Dih* would look in favor upon his quarter-blood godchild that night; for in his deafened, blinded condition he could do little or nothing more to save himself.

Luck, or *Ka-Dih's* divine intervention, stayed with the Kid and guided home his bullet full into the center of the looming shape's chest. Such was the shocking force of impact of that one third of an ounce of soft lead ball, propelled by the exploding pressure of forty grains of black powder—giving a power unequalled in any handgun until the smokeless powder firing .44 Magnums made their appearance in the middle of the 20th century—that the shape, a big, well-built man, was literally flung backwards on being hit.

On landing, the Kid continued to roll until he felt branches scraping his body and knew he had gone under the shelter and cover of a bush. Two more shots blared out and he heard the lead hammer into the ground somewhere before him, but he did not fire back. To do so in his present condition would be the height of folly and the Ysabel Kid was never very foolish.

Slowly his eyes cleared and the ringing noises left his ears. Reaching up, he wiped the tears from his eyes and focused his attention on the remainder of the attackers. That had been as close a call as he could remember and he figured he could safely and happily spend the rest of his life without a repetition of those few seconds. A man might grow old before his time if he made a habit of tangling in such a situation—happen he lived through it to grow old that is. However, it seemed that his attackers had decided to call the game quits for the night. Having lost three of their number, the remaining pair were already heading off through the *bosque*, and unless the Kid's ears still played tricks, Dusty and Mark's bunches also cut back to where they came from on the run.

A few seconds passed and hooves drummed beyond the *bosque,* fading rapidly into the distance. For fifteen minutes with Indian-like patience, the Kid remained in cover, gun and knife ready to handle any comers. Silence lay like a heavy cloud on the land after the noise of the past seconds. Slowly the night noises returned as startled creatures of the darkness resumed the normal tenor of their existence. In all that quarter of an hour neither Mark nor Dusty called out in an attempt to discover if their good friend be alive or dead. They knew that even if alive the Kid would not give away his position by replying until he knew he could do so safely.

Overhead a common nighthawk plummeted from the heavens and scooped up a moth which moved too slowly.

Nearby a cotton-tail rabbit screamed piercingly as a weasel jumped it. The Kid slid from under the bushes where he landed in his wild leap for safety. Still ready to shoot, he moved towards the first of his victims. Caution was not needed for the man lay dead, hit under the chin by a bullet which ranged up and ripped off his hat as it burst through the dome of his skull. The Kid noted this as he struck a match and illuminated the dead face.

He saw more—and what he saw sent him to the other bodies in a hurry.

CHAPTER THREE

Discovery at Dawn

"They're all Injuns, Dusty," said the Kid, sounding as if he did not believe the evidence of his eyes. "Both in the *bosque*, and out by the hosses."

After making his discovery of the identity of the attackers, and another which surprised him even more, the Kid returned hurriedly to the camp, announcing his coming with a low whistle both his friends would recognize. Leaving Dusty and Mark to get out and check on the results of their shooting, the Kid went to where his huge white stallion stood bristling in fury over the hideous thing which had once been a living human being. He calmed the horse down and led it clear of the body, then returned to examine the remains. Lighting a match on the seat of his pants, the Kid used its glow to study the results of the stallion's defensive assault. Even the Kid's Comanche-touch stomach felt a mite queasy at what lay before his eyes. However, he could make out enough from the bloody wreck of a body to determine that it, like the three he had found in the *bosque*, was an Indian—but the knowledge only deepened the puzzle.

"I must've only wounded the two I hit," Dusty put in. "There's no sign of bodies out where they shot from."

"One I got looked like a Kaddo to me," Mark drawled. "Tall and slim like they tend to be—and an Indian for sure."

"That's what I don't figure," stated the Kid. "Up in the *bosque* I dropped two Southern Cheyenne and a Pawnee, and ole Blackie done stomped a Teton Siouxdown or I've never seen one."

"There's all four tribes on reservations in the Nations," Dusty pointed out, although he could guess at what puzzled the Kid.

"Sure and most of 'em's been enemies from way back," the Kid replied. "Old tribal hate dies hard. No bad-hat Teton'd ride with a Pawnee——"

"Only?" Dusty queried.

"Only them bunch don't dress like bad-hat brave-hearts trying to get back the good old days. If anybody'd ask me, I'd say they was Mission School Injuns, all of 'em. White man suits, hair cut short, and not wearing paint."

No self-respecting Indian warrior would think of going into battle without first donning his medicine war paint to let the Great Spirit know where to aim good fortune. However, no self-respecting Indian warrior fought at night— and if he did chance it, ought to have done a far better job of the attack.

"They were all young cusses too," the Kid went on. "Sort who've got sense enough to know they're better off in the Mission School, so stay there, eat well, learn the Good Book—what they believe of it—and don't go raiding."

"Only this bunch did go," Mark reminded him.

"I yield to the gentleman from the Big Bend," answered the Kid. "And likewise agree with him that they done started raiding."

"Which brings up a right smart question," Dusty drawled. "Why did they start raiding?"

"Happen you think up a good answer," said the Kid dryly, "tell me 'n' Mark all about it."

"Now don't you go fretting none about *that*, Lon," Mark told the dark young man. "Happen he does, he will."

"Why don't you pair light the fire and brew some coffee happen you want to sit and whittle-whang this thing out?" Dusty inquired.

Clearly none of them would get any sleep until the Kid cleared his craw of the puzzling aspects of the raid. Both Dusty and Mark knew that, and, if the truth be told, felt just as curious to try to work out the peculiar facts which came to light after the guns stopped roaring. While neither claimed to have the Kid's encyclopaedic knowledge of things Indian, both knew enough to be pulled by certain aspects of the affair.

"Go get the wood, Lon," Mark said, in the tone of a martyr asking a friend to take first crack at becoming lion-fodder. "I'll fetch up the water."

"Don't go shooting any pronghorns," Dusty warned.

"That's not Lon's or my game," answered Mark pointedly. "We're—Hey! Over to the west—Look!"

Turning, the other two followed the direction of Mark's pointing finger. The storm, which had died down in the south, did not touch the western side of the horizon, yet out there something glowed redly in the sky.

"Fire," grunted the Kid.

"Never!" snorted Mark sarcastically.

"Fair sized one," Dusty put in. "Too far off for us to do anything about it anyways. Might have been caused by lightning."

"Won't do much hurt, way the wind is," the Kid guessed. "Just blow down to the south and storm'll douse it, if it's only a grass blaze."

"Where's Belle's place, Lon?" Mark asked.

"Down to the south, that glow's not from it. What'd you reckon she was keeping a lamp burning in the window for you?"

All three had thought of another, less harmless and innocent cause of the glow; a house or barn fired by Indians. However, they knew that long before they could reach the fire, all would be in order. Families were not so far scattered in this section of the Indian Nations that help would not be at hand quicker than the three Texans could make it.

"I'll fetch up some wood," the Kid said.

Fifteen minutes later the three friends sat around a fire of their own, while the glow to the west died down as mysteriously as it came. The coffeepot bubbled on the flames and the Kid opened the ball.

"Now with the Injuns I know," he said, "they either go to war to loot and count coup on the white-eye brother 'cause he's done lied and cold-decked them into a tizzy. Or some young buck wants to show how snuffy he is, so he gathers up a bunch of his *amigos* and they take out just looking to prove to everybody how the Great Spirit smiles on his fair-haired fighting sons."

"Or so's they can steal a bunch of horses to buy a wife with instead of courting the girl all loving and proper," Mark suggested.

"That too," agreed the Kid. "Only whatever way causes them to go, they go with their own tribe and they don't make war by night."

"Could've been fixing to surround the camp and hit us at the first sign of light," Dusty remarked. "That's always been good sound Indian tactics."

"Yep," agreed the Kid. "Could have been that way— only it sure as hell don't start to tell us how come Kaddo, Southern Cheyenne, Teton Sioux and *Pawnee* all come to be riding together."

"Hell, the fighting tribes have joined," Mark objected. "We've seen Yaqui out of Mexico riding with Mescalero Apaches, and the Cheyenne and Sioux teaming up to handle ole Yellow-Hair Custer on the Little Big Horn."

"And you once told us how your grandpappy cut arms and mixed blood with the Kiowa chief, then joined him to jump the Spanish settlements," Dusty went on.

"Sure," answered the Kid. "The *fighting* tribes did sometimes get together. A big name chief like Grandpappy Long Walker'd pay a visit to the leader of another tribe and ride along happen the other had him a fight going handy. But the Pawnee have been friends to the white man since back in the days of the mountain men and the fur trade. No *fighting* Indian'd trust tying hisself up with even a renegade Pawnee buck."

"Never sew a Mission Injun was worth a cuss as a fighting man anyway," Mark stated, reaching for the handle of the coffeepot. "Reckon it's the religion that spoils them."

"Could be," grunted the Kid. "What'll we do about this lot, Dusty?"

"There's not much we can do tonight. I don't reckon they'll be back again after the mauling they took, so we'll catch up on some sleep. Comes morning we'll take a good look at the bodies, see what we can learn. I reckon the living Indians have taken all their horses so we can't take the bodies with us."

"Got nothing to dig graves with," the Kid pointed out, not without a hint of satisfaction, for no cowhand cared to work on the blister end of a shovel.

"Wouldn't bury them even if we had," Dusty replied. "We'll leave them on top so the Army, or the nearest Indian Bureau agent can come out and look them over. He may recognize them."

"Where's the nearest reservation agency, Lon?" asked Mark.

"Down to the south, past the Starr place. About two miles from Lubbock. It's the big agency near Fort Hacken, the one with that fancy Indian college in it."

"We'll call in on the Starrs on the way down," Dusty told the other two. "Then Lon and I'll go on to Lubbock, report to the county sheriff, that'll leave you free to see Belle, Mark."

Mark and the Kid nodded their agreement. Following

Dusty's arrangements would allow them to kill two birds with one stone. While Mark saw Belle and learned why she sent such an urgent message to him, Dusty and the Kid could attend to the formalities; report the attack on their camp, present its facts to the authorities and maybe have the senior Indian Bureau official offer suggestions to clear up the puzzling aspects of the affair.

Dawn found the three Texans on their feet and examining the bodies. All had been lawmen and handled the work of searching the bodies thoroughly, if with some distaste. Although they went through the pockets of the dead Indians, they found nothing that might shed light on the reason for the attack. No money, no letters, which did not surprise the three Texans, but one significant thing which added to the mystery.

"Not one of 'em carrying any medicine pouch along," the Kid said. "Store suits, shirts, neck-ties. Hair cut short. And they're all wearing white man's boots. Lordy, lord, this gets worse by the minute."

Bending, Mark took up one of the Springfield carbines and turned it over in his hands. Like most Indian weapons, it bore a brass tack decoration on the woodwork—the glinting seen by the Kid during his fight in the *bosque*. However, Mark was less interested in the decorations than in a significant fact.

"Never saw Indians leave their *amigos'* guns behind before, even if they had to pull out and leave the bodies."

Dusty and the Kid gave their agreement to Mark's statement, and all three pondered on the deepening mystery.

"Want for me to take after the others and trail 'em down?" said the Kid.

"Reckon it'd do any good?" asked Dusty.

"Maybe. Only they went down to the south."

"The storm's over now," Mark pointed out.

"Sure," agreed the Kid. "But it was still going when they ran."

Which meant, as all three knew, that any sign of tracks would have been washed out by the rain.

"Why waste time?" asked Dusty. "We'll leave it until we've seen the Army commander and the Indian Bureau. This thing cuts deeper than we know."

Knowing Indians as only one with red man's blood in his veins could, the Kid agreed with Dusty. Much of the dark youngster's childhood had been spent around the camp of Long Walker's Comanches and he grew up with the teachings of his grandfather's lodge brothers to guide his knowledge of Indian matters. So the Kid knew even more than his friends just how wrong the attack had been. No Indian, even one debased by Mission School training, would make war without either war medicine or paint. Nor would any Indian fight in the night for fear that the Great Spirit might fail to find and guide to the Happy Hunting Grounds a warrior who fell in the darkness. Even if driven away during an attack, the Indian always tried to carry off any dead or wounded and never failed to try to take off the field any firearms no longer needed by killed companions. Yet these Indians who struck at the Kid's party had gone against every one of these things.

"Carried their shells loose in their pockets," Mark went on. "That stops us learning from the boxes where they got the bullets."

"It does," Dusty replied. "Collect all the guns, then let's ride."

Once in the saddle and riding away from the spring, Dusty, Mark and the Kid let the subject drop. No amount of rechewing over what they had seen would make the affair clearer. So they put it aside until such time as they could lay it before the authorities. The bodies had been left where they fell, faces covered over and some item of clothing hung flapping in the breeze, a sure method of scaring off coyotes, turkey-vultures or most other scavenging creatures. Having taken that precaution, and being unable to take the bodies along, the three friends headed south to visit the Starr ranch, then report the attack to the authorities.

The land they passed through was fine, open, rolling country much like the cattle ranges to the south. As yet the Indian Nations had not become over-populated and its soil so greedily worked that erosion had set in and created a hideous dust-bowl. While supposedly reserved as dwelling ground for the various transplanted Indian tribes, this section of land, the strip along which the north-bound trail herds passed, was settled by white men, small ranchers and nesters. It had been a good arrangement, the white settlers developing the land as no Indian could and acting as a buffer state between the red man and the passing trail herds. No Indian could see a trail herd without being reminded of the now-departed buffalo herds and trying to go back to the good old ways of cutting out what meat they wanted—no Texas trail boss would mildly allow a bunch of war-whoops to take animals from his herd without causing considerable fuss and burning of Du Pont black powder. So the white settlement of the trail drive route had been smiled on by those responsible for the peace of Oklahoma Territory. A fifty-mile-wide strip of choice land across the Indian Nations was left in the hands of white folks and everybody was apparently happy at the arrangement.

Two miles fell behind the horses and they came at last to the start of the area soaked by the previous night's storm. None of the trio had said much for the last mile, all being busy with their own thoughts. At last the Kid gave a grunt, shoved back his Stetson with a thumb and gave the pack-horse's hackamore a gentle pull. In addition to its normal

load, the horse now carried the dead Indians' carbines, but
was not over-loaded. The Kid glanced right and left and his
friends and his thoughts turned to their social problems.
Since the death of Comanche Blake's daughter, the only
girl the Kid had ever loved,* he had come to regard himself
as a confirmed bachelor. So he figured to give Dusty and
Mark something of a warning before they went and did
something plumb foolish. While the Kid thought both Freddie Woods and Belle Starr real fine ladies and damned good
women, he had no wish to see two first-water fighting men
lost to humanity because they were likely to be *loco* enough
to get all hawg-tied by marriage.

With the good of humanity in mind, and the purest of
intentions in his heart, the Kid started to sing, his pleasant,
untrained tenor giving forth a stern warning of the evils to
come.

"Now talking of women, you never can tell,
Sometimes they're heaven, but mostly they're hell.
Now first I loved a Kansas gal who damned nigh drove me
        crazy,
For at a dance she wouldn't prance, she was so fat and
        lazy.
A Mexican gal next took my heart, but it all ended sadly,
She carried a knife in her stocking top, I cut my hand quite
        badly.
A gal I loved in Taos town made me think I'd never roam,
I'd still be up in Taos town, but her husband done come
        home."

The song went on through all its forty-two verses, all
designed to prove that women are most undesirable and

*Told in *Gunsmoke Thunder*, by J. T. Edson.

untrustworthy creatures, and finished with a typical male sentiment.

"A bachelor's life is the life for me, no gal I'll try to tame. A bachelor's life is the life for me, and my sons'll be the same."

"Spoken like a dead mean Comanche," stated Dusty as the song came to an end.

"They're all the same," Mark went on. "Fact being, happen all Comanches think the same way as Lon, I'm surprised they ever get around to having any little Comanches!"

"We manage *that*," answered the Kid.

They were riding through a wooded valley now, on a day which made a man feel good to be alive. After the storm, the sky bore that clear, bright blue look which invariably followed dirty weather, as if trying to make up for the wetting of the previous night. Everything seemed cleaner, brighter, happier that morning. A scissortail fly-catcher flitted through the air, its long, V-shaped tail trailing behind like a banner. Up the slope a pair of eastern kingbirds blasted their fury on some feathered invader of their chosen domain.

"Dang fool critters," Dusty said. "I've never seen so much trouble in small piles as them."

Both Mark and the Kid grinned and much the same thoughts passed through two heads. Eastern kingbirds might be small, but few denizens of the feathered world could come up to them for pugnacious nature and fighting spirit. In many ways the kingbirds reminded the two Texans of their *amigo* Dusty Fog. Neither bird nor man feared any foe, no matter what size the enemy came, and both possessed effective methods of handling any intruder who riled them. The only difference being that Dusty never looked

for trouble and the kingbirds went out of their way to find
it.

To the right of the trail a cock turkey gobbled, and hens
replied. All three Texans exchanged grins at the sound.

"Sounds like a big old tom," the Kid remarked, and went
on hopefully. "How about me taking after him and bringing
him in for supper?"

"No go," Dusty answered. "You're coming with us."

"He just don't like going near the Indian Affairs Bureau
jaspers in case they heave him on to a reservation," Mark
put in.

"Don't like going near crooks," grunted the Kid. "Which
same's what all that Injun Affairs bunch are."

"There are some good men among 'em," Dusty objected.

"Yeah?" sniffed the Kid. "Well, I've never seen them."

A crashing of wings, and several dark shapes lifting
through the trees to disappear over the slope's rim, heralded
the departure of the flock of wild turkeys. Letting out a low
grunt, for no domesticated bird ever tasted half as good as
its wild-reared kin, the Kid slouched in his saddle and regretfully gave up his hope of turkey hunting unstead of
visiting the Indian Affairs office in Fort Hacken. The Kid
had not been entirely joking with his comments about the
men who controlled the destiny of the reservation-held Indians, and always felt riled in the presence of a man he
knew to be mishandling and robbing the once-proud red
warriors. With the Kid to feel riled usually meant trouble
for somebody and trouble was a thing he wished to avoid
at that time.

So the three friends rode on side by side, talking as they
went, following a clearly marked trail which showed signs
of much use. Much to the Kid's concern, he regarded it as
a most ominous sign; Dusty insisted on telling another of
Freddie Woods' stories. From the way the Kid viewed the

situation, both Dusty and Mark had been bitten so badly that there would be little or no chance of recovery in either case. Mark had just finished telling them a story given to him during a lull in a love-making session with Belle Starr, and Dusty seemed determined that his girl should top Mark's in the matter of windie-spinning.

"It was at a big, fancy dinner," Dusty told his friends. "A duchess sat next to Freddie passed wind so loud she nearly blew the pictures off the walls. Anyways, the duchess saw everybody looking at her, so she turned to the butler who was passing and said, 'Stop it, James,' and he answered right up with, 'Very good, Your Grace, which way did it go?'"

This time his friends laughed, swinging their horses around a curve in the trail. It was the last time any of them laughed for quite a spell.

Even as they laughed at Dusty's story, the three young men rounded the bend in the trail and what lay before them wiped out their mirth and caused them to bring their horses to a sudden halt.

Ahead of the three Texans, lying sprawled face down upon the ground in the center of the trail, was a human body. It lay in that grotesque, slightly hideous, uncaring attitude death often left in its wake. To one side lay a Stetson, come away from its owner's head in falling. Blonde, femininely long hair sprayed out on the ground in a white pool. A yellow fish, oilskin slicker, prevented much of the body's shape from showing; beneath it men's levis trousers stuck out, ending in high-heeled, fancy-stitched boots. There were several small black holes in the fish, but no sign of blood.

Mark was first off his horse. While he tried to fight down the knowledge, he could almost guess what lay before him. Desperately he tried to tell himself that more than one woman in the Indian Nations wore men's pants and boots and had blonde hair; and that a girl riding out upon a stormy night would dress in a more protective manner than divided skirt or riding habit offered against the elements. It was no use. Mark knew, even as his legs carried him forward the dozen or so strides to the body, just what he would soon see. Knew it, and desperately tried to fight off the knowledge.

Dropping to his knees, Mark raised the body and gently turned it over. A beautiful face, still and calm in death, looked up at him.

"Belle!" he gasped and his friends would never forget the sound of his voice.

CHAPTER FOUR

We'll Get Whoever Killed Her

Suddenly the shock of the sight hit Mark, even though he all but knew the identity of the body. After his one word the realization twisted into his guts like a knife. Cradling the body in his arms, he tried to persuade himself that it was all a ghastly dream, that he would wake up and find Belle smiling through it at him.

For a long moment Dusty and the Kid stood in shocked silence. To Dusty's mind it recalled another such scene; when the Kid found the body of his murdered sweetheart down in Apache Country, New Mexico. Over the years, mutual dangers shared had given the trio a bond as close as any brothers; cut one and the other two bleed. Back by the burned-out ruins of the small ranch where Comanche Blake died had been bad enough, but all three Texans were expecting trouble then. Somehow, if possible, the present situation felt worse. A few seconds before, all seemed so good with the world, they made jokes, laughed and enjoyed life—then they turned the corner into death.

A shudder ran through Dusty's frame as he tried to take hold of his emotions and force cohesive thought to his brain. A raw, hollow ache seemed to fill him as he looked down at his giant *amigo* kneeling, cradling the body to his chest.

Something must be done, that Dusty knew for sure. Somehow they must make a start at discovering the identity of Belle Starr's killer. On three occasions while working as a town marshal Dusty found himself faced with a similar problem and knew how to begin the investigation. Only this time was different. Now the issue became personal. A man did not lightly toss aside his feelings when a good friend's girl lay dead, victim of a brutal murder.

"Think!" Dusty told himself, and later realized he must be speaking aloud. "For God's sake think!"

How had Belle been killed? At what time, roughly, did she come to die? Did worse than death claim the girl first? Who might wish to see Belle dead; and have the means to kill her?

Those vital questions must be answered. Slowly Dusty lowered his eyes to the shape Mark still cradled in his arms. The girl's back turned towards Dusty and he saw the scattered holes in the yellow material of the fish. Small holes less than a .36 caliber revolver would have made. Only one kind of firearm made such holes; a shotgun firing a charge of buckshot. No blood marred the fish's yellow material; but from the stiffness of the body and the way its hair hung damply, death came some time back. During the rains, the blood would be washed away as it seeped through the holes and on to the fish.

In that case Belle must have been riding through the storm. Only a matter of great urgency would have taken her out upon such a night. Dusty could almost see the scene in his imagination: lightning flashing, momentarily illuminating the rain-slashed trail through the trees; the blonde beautiful girl riding through the night on some highly important mission, her hair hidden under the Stetson and shape concealed by the impersonal protective bulk of the fish; a dark, shadowy shape appearing behind Belle, shotgun raising, flame flickering from its barrel at—he fought down the mind-conjured picture. Gritting his teeth, Dusty exercised all his will-power and forced himself to think rationally about the killing.

One glance at Mark told Dusty that his big *amigo* would be of no use for the time being, not until the shock of the discovery left him. Well, that was what one had friends for, to help out in time of distress and sorrow. So Dusty knew that he himself must take hold and lay to the work that needed doing.

How far apart were the holes on the fish? A shotgun's charge started to speak fanning out into separate balls of flying lead, on leaving the barrel; everyone with even a basic knowledge of firearms knew that. Back East various law enforcement bodies had already started the scientific work which would one day evolve into the study of ballistics; and experiment on many things, including tests to determine roughly how far a charge of shot spread at various distances. Dusty knew a man, now captain of detectives on the Chicago Police Department, and from this source, in letters, learned the latest developments in scientific investigation, including the results of the shot-spread experiments. With that knowledge he hoped to be able to form a rough estimation of how far back the killer stood.

Unimportant, academic almost to some eyes; but Dusty figured the knowledge might be useful. If Belle had been killed on that spot, the Kid would know roughly in what area to concentrate his search for sign that the killer left.

Silently Dusty moved around his big *amigo* and looked at the still shape cradled in Mark's arms. Fortunately the blond giant held the body with its face and bosom to his body and Dusty could see all the back. One, two, three; Dusty counted the punctures in the fish. Eleven in all, the usual buckshot load per barrel being nine balls. Although the holes lay scattered across the back and left side of the fish, from below the shoulder blade to the rump, Dusty estimated the killer fired from less than fifteen yards. Judging from the holes, the gun had patterned very well.

"God damn it!" Dusty's brain screamed. "That's *Belle Starr*, Mark's girl, you're looking at." And cold, chilling reason flashed back the answer. "We have to think about those things no matter who's involved."

Again a shudder tore through Dusty's frame. Then his will-power drove him to look once more at the wounds. After that he stood erect, eyes half-closed as he tried to re-picture how Belle lay as they turned the corner.

"We have to do something, Dusty," said a voice, and so strained was it that Dusty took a couple of seconds to recognize that the Kid spoke.

"Sure," Dusty answered, his voice as brittle and unreal sounding. "Go cut for sign, Lon. Wouldn't go much more than twenty yards either way."

Looking at the ground, the Kid silently cursed his luck. Normally the trail's surface would have been too hard to show any imprints made by passing travelers. However, the rains of the previous night so softened the hard-packed earth that it now offered a surface ideally suited for a track-reader—but the same rains also washed out the sign left by Belle and her killer. Nor could the Kid be sure of where to start his search, for he had no way of knowing in which direction the girl rode when death took her. Of course, she lay head towards them and face down, but that meant little. In the convulsion of agony as buckshot tore into her back, Belle could easily have twisted in her fall from her horse.

Deciding to assume that Belle rode in the direction she could expect Mark to come, the Kid walked back along the edge of the trail. He kept his eyes on the ground, missing nothing, bending to check any faint hint of sign in the hope of learning something useful in their quest for Belle Starr's killer. Slowly, with a Comanche's inborn patience, the Kid worked back along the trail for something more than twenty yards. He looked behind such trees as might offer shelter and hide a waiting killer from view, searching with eyes trained to locate the faintest sign—and found nothing.

Halting, the Kid stood for a moment and raised his eyes to the skies. Gone was the look of innocence. Gone the white man's blood. A pure Comanche Dog Soldier stood at the edge of the trail with his face pointing to the heavens.

"A sign, *Ka-Dih!*" he said in Comanche, then turned back to English. "Just one lousy lil sign's all I ask. Is that too much?"

Like Dusty said, a man had to believe in something— especially at a time like this.

Crossing the path, the Kid started to work his way back along the other edge. Yet as he moved he felt a growing conviction that his task would be hopeless. A big old cottonwood tree grew just ahead, trunk bulky and sturdy. A man wanting to remain hidden from the trail, yet still able to observe any passers-by, would be sure to regard that tree as being placed in position by providence. However, no sing could exist after such a st——

At that moment the Kid's eyes caught a tiny glitter of something metallic lying among the grass beneath the tree and catching the sun's rays. Small the glint of sun on metal might be, but not too small for the Kid's eyes to catch it and read its meaning. There should be no such glitter among the grass, and under the prevailing conditions, anything out of the ordinary demanded closer inspection. Bending forward, the Kid looked down at the grass, his fingers reaching to part the blades and expose the glittering object. At the same time his eyes saw another out of the ordinary color among the green, this time a dull red, some inches from the first. Taking up the two objects which so attracted his attention, the Kid turned them between his fingers and looked at them. Soaked by the rain, the red tubes of stiff paper still held their shapes even though the packing of gunpowder, wads and lead balls had been fired from them, the brass heads still firmly attached and not tarnished by long exposure to the open air.

A low hiss left the Kid's lips as he stood up and dropped his eyes again to the pair of empty shotgun shells in his fingers. Only by the greatest of luck did he happen to spot the faint glitter of the sun on one of the brass heads, otherwise he might have walked right by the spot and been none the wiser. Clearly the killer used the cottonwood as shelter while waiting for Belle to ride by.

Slowly the Kid raised his eyes to the sky. "Lordy lord!" he breathed. "Maybe there's something to this *Ka-Dih* business after all. Thanks, Great Spirit of the Comanche."

With that the Kid made a thorough search of the area, eyes working like furies in their attempts to find some added sign that might lead to the killer of Belle Starr. After five minutes the Kid regretfully concluded that the rain had washed out every trace. Once he found a sapling which looked as if the reins of a horse might have been knotted around it, but that told him little. If the killer came by horse—and there seemed little chance that he—or she— walked or used a buggy to reach the spot, the downpour prevented any sign showing. Slowly, reluctantly the Kid decided that *Ka-Dih* had done everything possible under the circumstances and knew he would find nothing more.

On his return to his friends, the Kid found that Mark still knelt cradling Belle's body in his arms and Dusty stood silently to one side. The small Texan walked towards the Kid, a question in his eyes.

"Found these," the Kid said, holding out the two shell cases.

Taking the two tubes, Dusty turned them so he could look at the brass bases and read the inscription carved there by the makers.

"Just ordinary Winchester ten gauge buckshot," he said, although he expected no more. "You can buy them over the counter in any store west of the Big Muddy damned near."

"Sure. Only there's nothing else. I looked real careful."

"You don't need to tell me *that*, Lon. Now we've got to move Belle back to her home."

"It won't be easy, Dusty," said the Kid quietly.

"I know," agreed Dusty. "But we have to do it."

"I'll get the hosses," suggested the Kid.

Leaving Dusty to handle Mark, the Kid walked towards the waiting horses. Dusty sucked in a deep breath and turned towards his kneeling *amigo*. Dropping the two empty cases into his pocket, Dusty went to Mark's side and laid a hand on the blond giant's shoulder.

"Mark," Dusty said to the other. "Mark, listen to me. We have to take Belle back to her home."

Dull, lifeless eyes lifted to Dusty's face. Mark's handsome features looked old and haggard, showing no understanding of the small Texan's meaning. Cold fear hit Dusty, for he had never seen Mark in such a condition of shock.

"Mark!" Dusty repeated. "We can't just stay here. We have to take Belle back to her place."

No reaction came. The Kid led up the horses and halted, looking helplessly at Dusty. For once in his life, the Ysabel Kid felt inadequate to handle a situation. So did Dusty, but the feeling spurred the small Texan to an increased effort and made him the more determined to succeed in breaking through the barrier of Mark's grief–inspired shock.

"Lon," Dusty said. "Bring Blackie up here."

"Sure," answered the Kid.

Knowing what Dusty required of him, even without needing to ask, the Kid led his huge white horse to Mark's side. Down on the Rio Grande during the Kid's wild, lawless youth, it had sometimes been necessary to transport a wounded and near helpless comrade on horseback. So the Kid taught his horse a trick which made easy the problem of getting the wounded one on to a saddle. An order showed that the white had not forgotten the trick, for it sank to its fore knees and stayed motionless.

With the horse ready for mounting, Dusty turned his attention to persuading Mark to get aboard. Knowing the blond giant would never relinquish his burden, Dusty made no move to do so. Instead he gripped Mark's arm, feeling the enormous bicep under the shirt.

"Take hold of yourself, Mark!" he ordered, his voice harsh and authoritative. "You've got to do it—for Belle's sake."

Probably nothing else could have sunk through to Mark's brain. Realization crept slowly into his eyes, his giant frame shook in a shudder of reaction. After a glance down at the cradled shape in his arms, Mark came to his feet and walked towards the kneeling white, supporting the body with no more effort than if carrying a baby. Mark swung into the saddle and the white stallion lurched to its feet. Having ridden horses since early childhood, Mark stayed in the rising stallion's saddle without any visible effort, or requiring to think of keeping his balance. At the white's head, the Kid spoke gently, soothing down his horse's objections to letting others than himself sit its back.

"All set, Dusty," said the Kid when sure his white would obey his order and not fight against its burden.

Turning, Dusty walked forward and caught the trailing hackamore of the pack-horse, which the Kid turned loose when fetching forward his white. Securing the hackamore to his saddlehorn, Dusty mounted the big paint. The Kid walked up to the bloodbay and gripped its saddlehorn, swinging astride. Although he landed ready for trouble, the big horse seemed to be aware of the situation and did not try to fight against the stranger on its back, but allowed the Kid to start it walking.

Already Mark had started the white stallion moving and the other two swung their horses on either side of the white. For a time they rode like that, silent, grim-faced and each deep in his own thoughts.

A sign from Dusty caused the Kid to slow down his horse and they allowed Mark to draw ahead of them. Turning his dark face, now a cold Dog Soldier's mask, towards Dusty, the Kid waited to hear what the other had to say. Yet Dusty did not start speaking straight away.

"We'll get whoever killed her," the Kid stated flatly.

"That we will, Lon," agreed Dusty. "No matter how long it takes, or who gets hurt, we'll get the killer."

Thinking back on his lack of success at finding sign, the Kid gave his attention to another matter.

"Just how the hell do we start to find out who done it, Dusty?" he asked. "There's nothing to help us."

"There's always something," Dusty answered. "Where did you find the shells?"

"Under the big old cottonwood down the trail a piece from where Belle lay. Only there was no sign under it, the rain'd been beating down that way. Found what could've been the marks of reins on a tree back from it, only I couldn't be sure if they was or not, or when they was made."

"It looks like the killer waited for Belle then," Dusty stated.

"Or somebody else, and Belle happened along. Might have been somebody wanting to rob a traveler and needing a hoss. Belle's hoss wasn't around."

"Could be," Dusty agreed. "Only I can't see anybody hiding out on the off chance that somebody might come along. You know Belle, she was smart, alert, near on as keen with her ears and eyes as you. Now, with the state of

the weather last night she wouldn't be riding unless it be
real important. And happen she rode out on something *that*
important, she'd not be riding with her eyes and ears closed."

"In that sort of weather even a Comanche might miss
something."

"Sure. But what I mean is this. Suppose she came riding
along and found somebody on the trail, she'd be alert, ready
for trouble, and wouldn't just ride on by without watching
her back."

"The killer hid behind a tree," the Kid pointed out.

"And *waited*," Dusty went on. "How far off could anybody see or hear a hoss coming in a storm like last night?"

"Not far, down there among the trees and with the way
that trail winds about in blind corners."

"So the killer couldn't have heard or seen Belle coming
and waited on the odd chance."

"Likely," grunted the Kid.

"Which means whoever killed Belle knew she was coming this way and laid for her, doesn't it."

"Most likely," conceded the Kid.

"Then," Dusty said, his voice hard and deadly, "we've
got us a start. All we have to do is ask questions."

Silence again for several minutes. The pack-horse slowed
slightly and its hackamore tightened on the Kid's leg. Turning, the Kid prepared to handle the situation, but his eyes
went instead to the small Texan. "Belle was born and raised
down here in the Nations. She'd known Injuns as friends
ever since she was a kid and know's 'em like I do. Maybe
she heard about that raiding bunch, rode out figuring to
warn us—only one of the Injuns got to her first."

"Why'd she figure they'd jump us at the spring?"

"Because she knowed Injuns, and us. That spring's known
as a nighting–spot for trail herds going north and folks
coming south. Three nights out of any week you'd likely

find folks nighting there. And don't tell me the Injuns haven't got that figured out. If they wanted to raid, that'd be one place they'd go looking for folks, it'd be safer than hitting at a ranch house. Belle knew we'd be riding as soon as Mark got her word and that we'd be at the spring last night. So she come out to warn us."

While the Kid put up a real good case, Dusty spotted a couple of flaws in his friend's line of thought.

"That feller was waiting for her to come along. I'm sure of it," he said. "And Belle was killed with a shotgun. None of the bunch who jumped us had a ten gauge. Even if we'd missed the difference in sound between a shotgun and a carbine, we'd sure as hell noticed the difference in the muzzle-blasts."

"That's for sure," groaned the Kid. "Hell, Dusty, I don't know what——"

The Kid's words chopped off as he saw his big white stallion come to a halt. Throwing back its finely-molded head, the stallion's nostrils flared and it looked up in a manner Dusty, the Kid and, at another time, Mark recognized. Two hands moved. First a bone-handled Peacemaker Colt left its holster, and a good half-second later a Dragoon slid clear of leather. Both Dusty and the Kid knew that the white's training included giving warning of the presence of hidden danger.

"I'll take it!" said the Kid and left the bloodbay's saddle in a bound that carried him into the bushes flanking the trail, disappearing silently in the direction his own horse stared.

"Get ready to run for it, Mark!" Dusty ordered, riding to his big *amigo's* side and knowing the other would never drop his burden even if doing so might save his own life.

A minute passed, then a whistle came from the bushes. Although the whistle sounded just like the call of a kiskadee flycatcher, Dusty knew the bird never came so far north and also that the Kid sometimes used the call. One glance at Mark told Dusty the other could be relied on to think and act without guidance. So Dusty swung from his saddle and left the paint standing with trailing reins—all a range-trained horse needed to prevent it straying—then headed for the Kid's whistle.

Coming through the trees, Dusty found the Kid by a fine-looking, though lame, brown gelding. Moving forward, Dusty joined his dark friend and they looked the horse over with knowing eyes. The cause of the lameness showed plain; some half-a-dozen small wounds in the croup and thigh at the left side. Holes both Texans recognized as being caused by buckshot balls.

"Belle's horse," Dusty said quietly. "It threw her and ran when the lead hit. Then swung off and started back towards its home. Only the pain finally stopped it."

"That's how I read it," agreed the Kid.

"Which lets out the idea that somebody killed her for her horse."

"Reckon so. What now, Dusty?"

"I'll go and start Mark heading back to the Starr place, Lon. Or do you want to do it while I tend to the horse?"

"Get going. I'll see to it."

After watching Dusty ride away, the Kid gave a long, low sigh. With the air of a man about to perform an unpleasant task, the Kid started to remove the brown's saddle, before he put the animal out of its misery.

CHAPTER FIVE

Couch's Mistake

Range-raised though she was, Mrs. Starr almost went into hysterics when she saw the three Texans arrive and recognized that stiff shape in Mark's arms. Although managing to keep some kind of control on himself, Belle's father sank into a state of shock which prevented himself doing anything to help with his wife.

Everything fell on to Dusty's shoulders and, as usual, he handled the affair with quiet competence. Firstly he and the Kid took the grief-stricken parents into the house. Then Dusty drove Mark's unresponsive mind into action, forcing the blond giant to dismount and carry Belle's body inside, upstairs and lay it upon the bed in what had been the girl's room. After that, Dusty led Mark down into the sitting-room and left the big Texan seated at the table, staring ahead blindly.

After sending the Kid to the Starr family's nearest neighbors in search of assistance, Dusty went back into the house. Going up to Belle's room, he entered and closed the door behind him. Much as he hated the task, he started to perform the work of a lawman faced with such a problem. Unbuttoning the fish, he looked inside and saw with something close to relief that the clothing underneath appeared to be undisturbed. From all appearances the killer had not touched Belle after she fell from her saddle, so Dusty checked the contents of her pockets. He found nothing to even give him a start at locating her killer.

On leaving the bedroom, Dusty went downstairs and to the kitchen. Looking inside, he found the Starrs at a table and one look told him questioning them about Belle's movements must be put off until later. Neither would be able to help him in their present condition, so he left them to their grief and went outside to await the Kid's return.

From the look of the white stallion the Kid had wasted no time on the two mile ride to the Kissel place. He brought back Mrs. Kissel and her two daughters in their buggy, while one of their hired men rode after the party. Apparently the Kid had introduced himself and told Mrs. Kissel something about the situation for the plump, grey-haired woman came straight to Dusty on her arrival.

"Lord, what a shock, Cap'n Fog," she said. "Such a beautiful girl. Who killed her?"

"We don't know, ma'am," Dusty answered. "Reckon you'd best go straight to the house. The Starrs are taking it bad."

"I'll tend to them for you," she promised and walked away with her daughters following on her heels.

After the women entered the house, the Kid came to Dusty's side followed by the Kissels' hired man.

"Herb here allows there's been a mite of trouble around and about last night, Dusty," remarked the Kid.

"Sure was, Cap'n," agreed the lanky hired man, showing interest mingled with surprise at discovering that the Rio Hondo gun wizard was so small a man. "Pills Pilsen's best bull got out of his barn and run over a cut-bank, bust its fool neck. Bennet's corral gate done come open and his four brood mares took to running, one of 'em heavy in foal. Running didn't do her no good, he had to down her. There was Dutchy Deiter, he had him a dam bust, flooded out a growing of prime alfalfa."

"And there was that fire we saw down to the west last

night, Dusty," the Kid went on.

"Brehn's place," Herb confirmed. "His hay barn went up."

Dusty and the Kid exchanged glances, remembering their own troubles on the previous night.

"What're folks making of it?" Dusty asked.

"Indians," answered Herb. "Fact being the boss went over to the Agency with Pilsen and Bennet to see about it."

"Might be as well if we rode over there, Dusty," suggested the Kid.

"Might be, Lon. Go cut two horses out of the corral and I'll tell the folks at the house."

Leaving the Kid to care for his horse—Dusty had attended to his paint, Mark's bloodbay and the pack-horse while waiting for the Kid to return—Dusty returned to the house. Mark still sat at the kitchen table, his head resting on his hands. To one side stood the two Kissel girls, watching Mark with pity in their eyes. Hearing Dusty enter the room, the elder girl turned towards him.

"We're going to town," Dusty told her.

"How about your friend?"

"Leave him to me."

"He's Mark Counter, isn't he?" asked the younger girl.

"Yes'm."

"Belle said she was going to m——"

"Hush your mouth, Tildy Mae!" gasped the elder sister. "Go and ask Momma if she wants you to do anything."

Indignantly the elder girl hustled her sister from the room, then she came back to where Dusty stood at the table.

"The killing has to be reported," Dusty said. "Lon and I'll see to it."

"And Mark?"

"Just leave him be. He'll need time to get his feet again."

"I'll go fetch you both a cup of coffee."

After the girl left the room, Dusty looked down at Mark. "Will you be all right until we get back, *amigo?*"

Mark lifted his grief-filled eyes and for almost a minute stared blankly at Dusty. Then slowly recognition came and Mark answered, his voice harsh and unreal.

"Sh—She's dead, Dusty!"

"I'm sorry, Mark," Dusty replied, knowing how inadequate the words sounded but unable to think of anything better.

"She's dead——"

"Easy, Mark," Dusty said gently. "Listen, we have to ride into town to report it to the sheriff. Do you want to come with us?"

A long, shuddering sigh left Mark's lips and he shook his head. "I'd best stay on here, Dusty, with—her."

"If that's the way you want it. Go upstairs and rest for a spell. Come on, I'll go with you."

Gently Dusty helped Mark to rise and guided his friend's halting steps to the stairs. Mrs. Kissel appeared and helped as best she could, directing the two Texans into an empty room along the passage from where Belle's body lay. In the room Mark flopped on to the bed and lay looking up at the ceiling.

"Mark," Dusty said and his friend's eyes turned towards him. "When the sheriff comes, he'll be bringing the county coroner out. You know what that means?"

"I know," came back the low, bitter answer.

"You won't stop him?"

Once more the shudder ran through Mark's giant frame, for he knew full well what Dusty meant and hated the thought of the coroner performing his duty upon the beautiful body. However, cold reason took hold and Mark knew he must not interfere with something, no matter how he hated it, that might help them find the man who killed Belle.

"Just leave me be, Dusty," he said hoarsely. "I'll be all right soon."

"Sure, Mark. I'll see you when I come back."

"How's he taking it?" asked the Kid as Dusty walked from the house.

"Bad. But he's coming out of it."

"It was easier for me, Dusty. At least I could get started straight after the bastards who killed Comanche. Once we get started, Mark'll soon throw it off."

"He will," agreed Dusty. "There's nothing like revenge to take a man out of his grief. Let's ride."

Dusty and the Kid found no difficulty in locating the county sheriff's office on Lubbock's main street. However, only a tall, gangling deputy sat in the room, one foot hooked up on the desk top.

"What're you wanting Bill Duffin for, Cap'n?" the deputy asked. "He's done gone out to the Agency to try 'n' keep peace with the settlers and Tiltman, him being the chief agent."

"We came in to report a murder," Dusty replied.

Instantly the deputy brought his foot from the desk top and the lethargy fell away from him.

"Who was killed?"

"Belle Starr."

Shock came to the deputy's face. Any murder was bad, but the victim being a beautiful, talented, well-liked—Belle never committed any crimes in the Indian Nations or gave the law of Lubbock County cause to seek her in a professional capacity—girl made the crime far worse.

"Who done it?" growled the deputy.

"That's what we don't know," Dusty answered, "yet."

"She's a friend of your'n."

"A *good* friend," confirmed the Kid.

Swivelling his eyes towards the Kid, and seeing the expression on the Indian dark face, the deputy could almost feel sorry for Belle Starr's killer when the two Texans laid hands on him.

"We'll tell the sheriff for you," Dusty said.

"Thanks. I'll head straight out there and take Doc Leach with me."

Despite the man's lethargic appearance, Dusty reckoned that the first stages of the investigation could be left in his hands. So Dusty and the Kid took their borrowed horses and rode from town in the direction of the Indian Agency. Two miles beyond the city limits they came to a ford in a wide stream and beyond stood a sign announcing that the stream marked the boundary of the Fort Hacken Reservation.

"This's Injun country now," drawled the Kid as they crossed the stream.

"Sure," Dusty agreed. "Let's get on to the Agency."

After riding for half a mile the two Texans came into sight of the Agency, a cluster of large wooden cabins backed by smaller shacks in which lived the Indians assigned to the tender mercies of the agent in that particular area. Dusty and the Kid rode towards the second largest cabin before which stood a bunch of white men, local settlers from their appearance. To one side, cradling their tack-decorated Springfield carbines, a quartet of Indian reservation police-men watched the white intruders with impassive eyes. On the cabin's porch, shoulder against one of its supports, stood a big, burly man with shoulder-long red hair and an aquiline-nosed, dark Indian face. The man wore the blue cavalry tunic and trousers and moccasins of the reservation police, had three stripes on his sleeves, and a gunbelt supporting a long barrelled Cavalry Peacemaker butt forward at his right side. There was a hint of sullen arrogance about the man, truculence showed in his pose and face as he looked down at the group of settlers.

Few eyes turned to the newcomers so Dusty and the Kid

dismounted and let their reins trail. Pop Starr bred and trained horses, his animals could be relied upon to stand when range-tied. Leaving the Kid to take the bundle of carbines from behind his saddle. Dusty walked by the crowd and towards the cabin. A sign on the door announced that the building was the adobe and office of Oscar G. Tiltman, Chief Agent for the Fort Hacken Reservation.

"Where'd you reckon you're going, boy?" growled the burly man on the porch.

"Into the office," Dusty answered.

"They're real busy inside," said the man, a thin sneer flickering on to his face. "Got too many folks inside right now."

"This's important."

"So's what all them lot there want to say, only they can't come in neither."

"Watch him, cowboy," said a low voice from among the settlers when it became obvious that Dusty did not intend to stop. "That's Will Couch."

"I aim to go in there, *hombre*," Dusty warned, showing no sign that the name meant anything to him. "My business's real important."

"And I'm here to stop folks going in," answered Couch. "Important or not."

Although Couch's name meant nothing to Dusty, the small Texan disliked the man's tone and attitude. Racial prejudice did not enter into Dusty's feelings; the fact that the other was a half-breed meant nothing. What Dusty objected to was the man's sneering tones and general manner. Clearly Couch did not care how important Dusty's business might be, or what the business concerned. All the man aimed to do was show off his superiority over the white folks who came on to Indian land.

Dusty had neither the time nor the inclination to be delayed or shown.

Seeing that Dusty did not intend to stop, Couch gave thought to his position in life and reputation as a real hard man. Things looked mighty favorable for the elevation of Couch's dignity. First, four reservation police stood at hand ready to hold back the other white men; second, inside the cabin were influential people, one of whom would always believe any story told by an Indian or half-breed and discount the words of her own kind; thirdly, no white man would risk starting gun-play on reservation land and against an Indian; lastly, and most important, the Texan looked so small and insignificant that he would fall an easy victim to Couch's brute strength. With all that in his favor, Crouch reckoned he could handle the Texan and impress the watching crowd with his superiority over the white race.

However, Couch never took chances at such times. So he intended to lull the Texan's suspicions and then fell the small intruder before the other realized what happened.

"All right," he growled. "Come ahead."

With that, Couch stepped to Dusty's right side, giving the impression that he aimed to let the small Texan pass by. Then, as Dusty came alongside, Couch swung up his right arm, intending to crash it into the small Texan's chest and knock him backwards from the porch. So confident in his strength over the small Texan's was Couch that he did not even try to hook his right leg behind Dusty to help throw him from his feet.

It was a good trick in Couch's class of fighting company; only doomed to miscarriage when the man failed, through ignorance of the facts it is true, to grasp one small but vital point.

Like many folks in the late 1870's, Couch had never heard of the Japanese islands or the strange fighting arts developed by the Nipponese race. Nor did Couch know that a member of that race lived in the Rio Hondo country, employed as bodyservant by Ole Devil Hardin; a man fully conversant with the mysterious art of karate and ju-jitsu. Not knowing that, Couch could not suspect that Tommy Okasi taught his secrets to the smallest of the Hardin, Fog and Blaze clan. Seeing the methods as an ideal method of off-setting his lack of inches, Dusty learned well; by present day standards his knowledge would have qualified him as fourth dan black belt in both ju-jitsu and karate. With that knowledge to back up his not inconsiderable strength, Dusty was hardly the easy meat Couch expected.

Even as Couch swung the blow towards Dusty's chest, the small Texan, who knew both attack and its counter, bent his legs and inclined his body forward. Keeping his right fist pointing upwards, Dusty blocked Couch's blow in the region of the elbow joint. In almost the same move Dusty brought up his left arm on the outside of Couch's trapped limb. Unclenching his right fist, Dusty linked fingers with his other hand. By pulling Couch's upper arm towards his right hip and pressing forward on the trapped wrist with his left shoulder, Dusty applied a painful lock against the elbow joint. Pain brought a cursing Couch to his knees, but he retained sufficient common sense not to struggle against the hold.

Seeing Couch's failure, the four reservation policemen started to move forward, hefting their carbines. The rescue attempt came to a sudden halt due to the Ysabel Kid's shrewd summing up of the tactical situation. Like most men in Texas, the Kid carried his rifle boosted low on the left side of the saddle, butt pointing to the rear; a position which allowed speedy withdrawal of the weapon. Without releasing the bundle of carbines from his left hand, the Kid gripped the butt of his rifle and slid it from the boot. Still holding the rifle one-handed, the Kid curled his fingers through the loading lever. Snapping his wrist, he caused the barrel of the rifle to tilt forward and down, which caused the mechanism to operate. When the barrel reached its lowest angle the breech lay open and as the butt counter-pivoted back into place, a bullet fed into the chamber. Clamping his thumb around the small of the butt, the Kid slid his forefinger into the triggerguard and stood full ready to cut loose should it be needed.

"Hold it!" he barked.

The words brought the four Indians to a halt just as effectively as did the unmistakable double click which heralded a round being fed into a Winchester's chamber, for the order came in a deep-throated Comanche grunt. Turning their eyes in the direction of the voice and sound, they found themselves covered by a Winchester that, although held one-handed, lined rock-steady for instant use. Being skilled rifle handlers themselves, even if forced to carry poor quality weapons, the policemen knew class when they saw it—and they saw it in that black-dressed, Indian-faced Texan who stood before them. Having no great liking for Couch, the policemen figured their gesture sufficient in that they made the effort, and saw no point in getting shot, which would be the only way they could take the matter further.

"All right," Dusty growled, still holding Couch's arm. "Call it off."

Low muttered curses answered the small Texan's request, then, "Leave be, cowboy, I quit."

Releasing Couch's arm, Dusty stepped clear of the man then waited, tense and ready to meet any further attack. Nor was his expectancy misplaced. Couch, down on one knee, lifted his face to the small Texan's. Hatred and fury glowed in the dark eyes and, with a snarl of curses leaving his lips, Couch hurled himself forward with his big hands reaching out to take hold of and crush the man who brought him to his knees.

A yell of warning rose from the watching settlers, who

had seen Couch in a fight and knew the danger of letting him lay hands on one at such a moment. Not one of the watching crowd fully understood just how Dusty averted the first attack, most attributed it to luck, and felt sure he would fall victim before the big half-breed's sudden rush.

In the face of the treacherous attack, Dusty lost his temper. The tensions of the past few hours welled up and smashed through like water out of a bomb-shattered dam. All the small Texan's pent-up emotions exploded and Couch caught the full benefit of the released fury.

Instead of trying to avoid the rush, Dusty went forward to meet it, gliding in and ignoring the yells of the local men advising him to stay clear. Fury or not, Dusty did not go blindly into the attack, but moved with deadly purpose. He held his hands in a manner which appeared strange, inadequate even, to eyes accustomed to more formal fighting men.

Up came Dusty's hands, fingers straight and tight together, thumb bent over the palm. The heel of each hand chopped into Couch's reaching forearms, knocking them away. Then with the speed that enabled him to draw and shoot a gun in less than half-a-second, Dusty drove out his left arm in the *yon hon nukite*, the karate four-finger thrust at the solar plexus. In such matters Dusty aimed as accurately as when he used his Colt. Couch felt his advancing body ram into what felt like a wedge of iron. The fingers sank deep into his body, exploding the wind from his lungs, halting his rush and causing him to start to double over.

Like a flash Dusty struck again, this time with his right hand. Although he bunched his hand into a fist, Dusty did not strike in the formal manner. Instead, his arm came around and up, lashing the back of the fist into the down-dropping face. In one way Couch might have counted himself lucky in that the blow caught and smashed his nose. A blow in the *uraken*, back fist manner, which drove the second knuckle into either the philtrum nerve collection just under the nose, or the spot in the center and below the bottom lip, could be fatal when coming at the power Dusty hit. However, Couch did not appreciate his luck. Agony ripped into him. The force of the blow lifted him erect and flung him backwards. One hundred and ninety pounds of hard fleshed human body hurled back and crashed into the door. Wood splintered and screws burst from the hinges. Couch and door together collapsed back into the agent's office.

"There's some'd say you knocked just a lil mite too hard, Dusty," remarked the Kid walking forward.

CHAPTER SIX

Stormy Meeting at the Agency

Some half-a-dozen settlers; one fat, pompous dude in town-style clothing; a tall, tanned, lean and range-dressed sheriff; two young men dressed in an eastern fashion, although one was clearly an Indian; and a woman, all came to their feet, staring at the shattered door and the groaning, weakly moving, sergeant of reservation police who lay upon it. Then slowly, every eye lifted to the small Texan as he entered the room, stepping over Couch's body.

"You take a heap of seeing, Sheriff," Dusty said, ignoring the Artillery Peacemaker in Bill Duffin's right hand.

"D—Did you do that?" gasped the fat dude, staring with bug-eyes from Dusty to Couch and back again.

"Couch didn't do it hisself, that's for sure," grunted the sheriff, holstering his Colt. "Howdy, Cap'n Fog. What brings you here?"

"What the hell happened?" yelped the fat man.

"Your hired man took a mite of persuading that I'd urgent business here," Dusty explained.

"I left orders that nobody was to be admitted until this meeting came to an end, Mr. Tiltman," the slim, sallow-faced young white man in eastern clothes put in.

"Which same that *hombre* tried real hard to tell me," Dusty went on. "Only he picked the wrong way to do it."

"And you objected to a *half-breed* telling you anything," hissed the woman.

Dusty turned his eyes to the speaker. Maybe at one time

she had been a real fine-looking woman, but advancing age left its mark on her. The red hair, though neatly combed, bore tinges of grey which not even henna could hide. At a distance her face looked attractive. Up close the skin was coarse and there were bags under the eyes. She still possessed a reasonable figure, but Dusty did not care to guess to what extent it relied on artificial aids to retain its shape. In fact Dusty found the woman's appearance of less interest than the expression of hatred on her face as she glared at him with cold, unfeeling eyes.

"I don't know what his being a half-breed's got to do with anything, ma'am," he stated. "I came here to see the chief agent and that *hombre* tried to jump and rough-handle me instead of listening to what I said."

"This happens to be a very important meeting with the various local land-owners, cowboy," Tiltman put in pompously.

"I represent the OD Connected, mister. Which they do tell is a fair piece of land for a man to own."

Even a dude reservation agent who knew little about the West could not help having heard of the OD Connected ranch, which covered more land than the combined holdings of all the assembled settlers. Tiltman was also painfully aware of the amount of pressure the owner of the OD Connected could bring to bear in high places. No minor government official, who could easily be replaced, ever cared to rile up Ole Devil Hardin, or even cross the rancher's representative. However, the OD Connected lay far to the south in Texas and Tiltman failed to see why its man should interest himself in Oklahoma affairs.

Not that Tiltman doubted Dusty's claim to be representative of the ranch, for Duffin mentioned a name known well enough to the Indian agent when greeting the small Texan. If further proof be needed, Couch's present condition gave it. Any man who could so handle and defeat the big sergeant—coming through the affair without a mark of injury—must be well above the herd, no matter how tall he stood.

However, the woman did not take a similar attitude. Glaring at the sheriff and pointing hostilely at Dusty, she said, "Aren't you going to arrest this man?"

"This here's Cap'n Fog, Mrs. Ford," Duffin protested.

"And does that set him beyond the law?" she demanded hotly. "Or is the assault on a mere, lousy half-breed of no importance?"

"It's no crime to defend yourself, ma'am," Dusty said gently.

"What happened, Cap'n?" asked Duffin before the woman could reply.

"I came to see the agent on mighty important business, which same I told that *hombre*. He said for me to come in, then tried to jump me when I went by. I held him easy the first time. When he tried it again, I reckon I got riled."

"Sure looks that way," said one of the settlers, grinning broadly and bringing an angry hiss from the woman.

"I've told Couch afore about mishandling folks," Duffin remarked.

"He only does his duty!" yelled the woman.

"So when Couch jumps a white cowhand and works him over, that's doing his duty," Duffin blazed back. "But when one of my deputies has to lay hands on some owlhoot, it's a case of brutality by a law officer."

"Now just a minute!" yelled Tiltman. "This's a meeting about those incidents last night, not a political slanging match."

"Then keep it that way," barked Duffin. "Tell your boys to take Couch to the post surgeon and I'll go out and ask those folks what happened—and afore you say it, Mrs.

Ford, I'll ask the reservation police first. Reckon you'll take an Injun's word, unless it's not what you want to hear."

"I'll listen to any *unbiased* reports. I always have."

A disbelieving guffaw rose from the listening men at the woman's words and her face turned even more red. However, Tiltman showed some diplomatic promise in the handling of an unpleasant situation.

"Mr. Ede," he said. "Will you and Mr. Three-Feathers take Sergeant Couch to his quarters. Sheriff, I think you'd better go and ask your questions. For the rest, I think we'll postpone the meeting for half an hour until all this is settled."

Moving forward, the two young men in the eastern-style suits directed scowls at Dusty and then helped the still-moaning Couch to his feet. Supporting the burly sergeant, they left the room. Mrs. Ford followed on the sheriff's heels as he passed out to start inquiring into the cause of conflict between Dusty and Couch. For a moment the bunch of settlers remained together, talking in low tones among themselves and darting glances in the small Texan's direction. Tiltman stood at his desk, gazing down at the papers on it, then jerked up his eyes to study Dusty. As if coming to a difficult decision, the agent came across the room.

"What brings you here, Captain?" he asked. "These gents came to complain about some trouble they had in the storm last night."

"That's what brought me here, too," Dusty replied. "I'll wait out my turn with the rest of them though."

"Did them damned Injuns jump your herd, Cap'n?" asked one of the settlers. "They opened up my corr——"

"That's not been proven!" Tiltman interrupted.

An angry rumble of protest rose from the men as they started to move forward. With his lawman's training, Dusty sensed danger. The men regarded him as a potential leader and surged towards where he stood with Tiltman, clearly aiming to force home their point of view.

"Just hold it, gents," he ordered, and gentle though his voice sounded, it brought the men to a halt. Westerners all, they knew that tone; it was from a man used to giving a command and having it obeyed. "We've come to see Mr. Tiltman here on business. We're in his office at his invitation. So that being the case, we'll play the game the way he deals it."

"All of us had trouble last night, Cap'n——" began a short, grizzled old-timer respectfully.

"So did I," answered Dusty. "But waiting until the sheriff and the others get back won't make things any worse."

As usual in such matters Dusty had his own way. The men fell back to their original place and started a low-voiced conversation among themselves. Mopping his brow, Tiltman shot a gratitude-filled glance at the small Texan. Things had been looking ugly ever since the arrival of the settlers and only Bill Duffin's presence prevented serious trouble. Tiltman had never expected co-operation from Dusty, so receiving the small Texan's support came as a pleasant surprise and made the agent more inclined to be friendly.

"What caused the trouble between Sergeant Couch and yourself, Captain?" he asked.

"I told you my side of it, see what the sheriff says when he comes back," Dusty answered. "Only you want to watch that *hombre,* he's trouble."

"I know," admitted the agent frankly, "but it takes a hard man to handle the reservation police."

"There're ways and ways of being hard. All this kind'll do is buy you bad trouble."

While not willing to admit it, Tiltman felt inclined to agree with Dusty. To give him his due, Tiltman was one of the few serious agents who tried to improve conditions and work for the betterment of his charges. However, he found difficulty in gaining the confidence of the Indians and keeping peace with the settlers. Years of near hostility and lack of interest had made both sides of the reservation boundary line suspicious of the other. The meeting that afternoon proved just how wide a gap lay between the neighbors.

The Kid had not followed Dusty into the room, but stood with his back to the wall, the carbines lying behind him and his rifle resting negligently over his arm. With Indian-like bluntness, he refused to answer any questions and ignored the excited chatter of the settlers, watching the reservation police with careful eyes. Nor did he attempt to move when folks came from the office. Duffin glanced in the Kid's direction in passing. So did Mrs. Ford, but, recognizing him as a Texan, did not waste time questioning him. She knew the Kid would lay all the blame, right or wrong, on Couch, which was not what she wanted to hear.

Unfortunately for Mrs. Ford, the reservation police still retained the Indian belief that a questioner expected to be told the truth. So she heard the plain, unvarnished, and to her unpalatable, fact that Couch started the trouble and made a treacherous attack on Dusty Fog. Flush-cheeked and angry, she started back towards the office with a faintly-grinning Bill Duffin on her heels. So delighted was Duffin at seeing Mrs. Bertha Ford thwarted that he failed to observe the bundle of carbines lying behind the Kid. However, before Duffin entered the office a surge of watching settlers brought him round.

"Ease off there, boys," he ordered. "We'll play her out the same way as before. Only the gents involved need come inside."

Tensing slightly, the Kid prepared to give Duffin his moral support, but did not need to. In his time as sheriff of Lubbock County, Duffin had built a reputation for fair play, but also as a man who would stand no nonsense when he gave an order. Backing off, the settlers stood clear and waited to hear what the men who actually suffered lost and damage the previous night had to say when the meeting ended.

"Well, Sheriff?" asked Tiltman as Duffin entered the office.

"Best let Mrs. Ford tell you," answered the sheriff, not without a hint of satisfaction in his voice.

Anger showed on the woman's face as she saw every eye swinging in her direction and read anticipation of the humiliation on almost every set of features. Dusty could almost feel sorry for her as red flushed into her cheeks and her lips drew tight with disappointment. In a voice brittle and throbbing with frustration and fury, the woman told Dusty his story had been confirmed. Then she stamped across the room to sit in one of the chairs behind Tiltman's desk. Seeing that the meeting would soon be starting again, the settlers took their seats and chattered among themselves, directing glances at the fuming woman as they talked.

"You've got a tolerable mean streak in you, Sheriff," drawled Dusty, in a low voice while the clatter of seating masked his words.

A grin flickered across Duffin's leathery face. "Reckon you don't know who she is, Cap'n. That's Bertha Ford. Name mean anything to you?"

"Yeah," agreed Dusty. "It means something."

Memory flooded back to Dusty and he recalled how three years previously, Bertha Ford's name had been prominent due to a series of articles published in various newspapers and telling of her "fact-finding" tours in which she "investigated" reports of army atrocities against the Indians, or exposed "brutalities" committed by law enforcement officers against poor, misunderstood criminals. As she had been crusading under the Radical Republican banner, her articles lost their party thousands of badly needed votes. Being a stout Democrat himself, Dusty did not object to anybody losing votes for the Republicans, but he despised the motives behind Bertha Ford's attacks. In her blind, misguided attempts to find some way to produce a stick and beat the Democrat dog, she maligned honest, hard-working men handling difficult, dangerous and thankless work.

Dusty felt surprised to see the woman, for in a letter his young friend Waco mentioned meeting the campaigning Mrs. Ford and that her teeth had been well and truly pulled.* Apparently she must have grown a fresh set, for here she sat and, if the sheriff's attitude be anything to go by, had gone back to her old ways once more.

"What's she doing out here?" he asked.

"Her, young feller called Ede and an educated Injun called Joe Three-Feathers come out here from the Injun College back East and started running a school for the young bucks. Know the thing, dress 'em up in white——"

Before the sheriff could go any further, the two young men in question returned from assisting the injured Couch away. Ede was tall, sallow-faced, with long untidy hair, handsome in a sullen way and well dressed. Although he wore town style clothes, stand-up collar and tie, city shoes, and sported short hair. Three-Feathers was pure Indian; tall, wide-shouldered and powerful in appearance. Studying the Indian, Dusty remembered that the bunch who attacked his party dressed in a similar manner.

"How's Couch?" asked Tiltman.

"His nose is broken," Ede replied, throwing a scowling glare at Dusty.

"I want to see him when this meeting is over," the agent

*Told in *Waco Rides In,* by J. T. Edson.

barked. "Now let's get down to business. I'd better explain, Captain Fog, all these men came here with reports of storm damage last night."

"Injun damage you mean!" barked a burly, white-haired man.

"None of you have proved that, or brought a single shred of evidence to support your claims," Mrs. Ford put in.

"Hell!" growled a short, wiry old-timer. "That storm washed out all sign."

"And could also have accounted for every incident," Ede said. "The scaring of the bull and horses could have been done by thunder or lightning, and lightning could have fired the hay barn. The wreck of the dam could have been caused by rising water due to the rain-fall. Apart from racial bias, there's not a thing to point to any human element being involved. Is there, Sheriff?"

"Hosses and cattle have been spooked by storms. Fires started by lightning, too, and rivers rising with rain've bust down dams," agreed Duffin. "Only when they all happen in one night, folks start to thinking things."

"And naturally they start blaming the Indians!" hissed Mrs. Ford.

Angry growls rolled up from the settlers and Duffin tensed, ready to move in to protect Mrs. Ford and her supporters should the men grow ugly. Dusty moved from the door, halting before the desk. Slowly he turned and looked at the settlers and silence fell on them as they waited to hear what brought him to the Agency.

"Like the lady said," he drawled. "Everything that happened to you gents might have come about through the storm. Only there wasn't any storm where we made camp last night——"

"And what happened, Cap'n Fog?" asked Duffin, interest plain in his voice.

"A bunch of Indians jumped us."

The quietly-spoken words created something of a sensation in the office. Talk welled up among the settlers; Tiltman opened his mouth, then closed it again; Duffin's face for the first time showed some expression as he studied the small Texan. For his part, Dusty watched the faces of Bertha Ford's party. Clearly Dusty's words had shaken them. Startled glances were exchanged; puzzlement showed on the two white faces, while the Indian retained his impassive mask except for a slight frown which creased his brow.

First to recover her composure was the woman. She turned cold, disbelieving eyes in Dusty's direction. "I suppose you have proof to confirm your statement; proof that it *was* Indians who attacked you."

"Just what kind of proof would you need, ma'am?" asked Dusty dryly.

"You wouldn't take prisoners, but no doubt you killed some of the attackers."

"Five and wounded maybe two more."

A low hiss left Three-Feathers' lips, drawing a scowl from Ede and a quick glance out of the woman.

"Where are these wounded?" she asked, turning back to Dusty.

"They got clear, with the rest of the bunch that jumped us."

"And the dead?"

"The bunch who ran took all the horses. We couldn't tote in the bodies and figured the sheriff, or the agent'd want to see them, so we left them out there."

"Then," the woman purred, "all the sheriff has to do is ride out and verify your story."

"That's the easiest way, ma'am. The sheriff, Mr. Tiltman here and a couple of folks *you* trust not to lie for us white men."

Once more the cold hate flickered into Bertha Ford's eyes as she detected the sarcasm which lay under Dusty's soft-spoken words. Fury drove her to speak without thinking.

"And if there are no bodies?"

"Then somebody'd best start in explaining where in hell these came from."

The Ysabel Kid had remained outside, watching the crowd and listening to the conversation. Timing his entrance to the right dramatic moment, he spoke up and walked into the room with his bundle under one arm. Winchester hanging in his other hand. Crossing to Tiltman's desk, the Kid laid the bundle on it, took out his bowie knife and slit the fastening then picked up and held out one of the track-decorated Springfield carbines.

Throwing over his chair, Tiltman came to his feet and pointed to the pile of weapons on his desk top.

"But . . . But they look like the guns my reservation police carry."

"It doesn't follow that they are," Three-Feathers put in. "I know the police do decorate their carbines in such a manner. But that is the traditional Indian way of warding off evil spirits."

"Probably hundreds of these carbines are in white men's hands," Ede went on. "Trophies of the Indian Wars and——"

"Just what're you getting at?" growled the Kid.

Studying the dark, dangerous face, Ede gulped, then took heart in the knowledge that Sheriff Duffin would protect him. "Only that these don't prove Indians attacked you."

"Easy, Lon!" Dusty snapped, catching the other by the arm and holding him. "The man's right, it doesn't prove a thing. So I reckon he'd best be one who comes out and sees for himself."

"Yeah," agreed the sheriff. "I reckon Mrs. Ford'd believe Injuns did it if you told her, *Mr*. Ede."

"How about the rest of us, Bill?" asked the burly settler.

"You and Bennet come with me," Duffin answered. "Others go back to town and wait until we get word—and stay out of the saloon. I'll jail any man who makes a fool move."

Every man present knew Duffin meant what he said, so none raised objections to his orders. On leaving the office, all but the two named by the sheriff took to their horses and rode out of the Agency area. Ede and Three-Feathers collected their mounts and trailed along behind Dusty, the Kid, Duffin and the two settlers as they rode out in the direction of the spring.

Only a little talk passed among the party as they rode. At the rear Ede and Three-Feathers spoke in low tones, ignoring the others. Dusty did not find an opportunity to tell Duffin of Belle Starr's murder, for the small Texan wished to be alone with Duffin when making his report.

Knowing the range, Duffin led his party by the shortest route to the spring, but from the first moment they came into sight of the water Dusty and the Kid knew things had gone wrong.

"Well," Ede sneered as he drew his horse alongside Dusty's mount. "Where are all the Indians you killed?"

Dusty did not reply, but the Kid, looking towards where one body lay when they pulled out that morning, gave a low grunt.

"Danged if somebody hasn't been here afore us and done snuck them all away," he answered.

CHAPTER SEVEN

She was Carrying a Child

Without another word, the Kid swung his horse and rode towards the *bosque* where his victims had been left. Pilsen, the burly settler, dropped from his saddle and bent forward, pointing to the crushed-down, springy grass, and a dark brownish patch of something that most certainly was not grass.

"This's blood," he said. "Something's been lying bleeding here, then was picked up and toted off."

Also dismounting. Three-Feathers examined the tracks. "No moccasins made these marks," he stated.

Give Pilsen his due, he agreed with the Indian's statement, then looked down at the town shoes the other wore.

"I've seen an Injun wearing white man's shoes," the settler growled.

"It's true I wear them," admitted Three-Feathers. "I learned at the Indian College back East. But none of the other men at our school have become accustomed to wearing other than moccasins."

"Which's true enough, Pills," Duffin put in. "I've seen those young bucks at the school wearing suits, shirts, ties, but never anything but moccasins. I reckon you'd best tell us all about it, Cap'n Fog."

Dusty dismounted and told the story of the attack, leaving out only how the attackers were dressed. Why he made the omission Dusty could not explain, but he saw relief creep into Ede's face, although Three-Feathers retained his stoic mask and showed nothing of his thoughts.

"There were a heap of things that looked wrong about the attack," Dusty finally admitted.

"It could be there was too much," Ede said.

"Meaning?" growled Duffin.

"You know there has been considerable agitation to take the Indians off their land and throw it open to white settlement?"

"So they say, Mr. Ede," agreed the sheriff.

"It's just possible that all these attacks were the work of white men, disguised as Indians, trying to stir up trouble."

"You admit there were some attacks last night?" asked Dusty.

"I admit nothing," Ede countered. "You all claim that there were incidents. All I'm doing is offering another explanation for them."

"You siding them red scuts against white folks?" growled Bennet.

"A man's entitled to his thoughts and say-so," Dusty pointed out. "All I know is that the attack didn't look like Indian work——"

Throwing a puzzled look in Dusty's direction, Ede said, "I only pointed out that the evidence suggests men disguised and acting as Indians."

"And the Ysabel Kid wouldn't know the difference?" asked Duffin.

"It *was* a real dark night, Sheriff," Dusty remarked quietly.

Swinging towards the small Texan, Duffin looked long and hard at the tanned face, yet failed to read anything from it. While being a smart lawman, Duffin found himself at a loss to decide just what Dusty intended by his words. However, having faith in Dusty's judgment of the situation, Duffin went along with the small Texan.

"Yeah," he said thoughtfully. "There's that to it."

"You saying that white men jumped you and you took 'em for Injuns?" barked Pilsen hotly.

"I'm only saying that we were jumped, no more, no less," Dusty replied. "We thought the attackers were Indians, only there was a lot about the attack that didn't look like Indian work. That's all I said."

For a moment Dusty and Pilsen locked eyes, but the big settler looked away first. From Pilsen, Dusty turned his attention to Ede and read something akin to relief in the young Easterner's eyes.

Before anything more could be said, the Kid returned. "They've gone," he said.

"Any sign?" asked Bennet.

"Some."

"Injun sign, or just what looks like it's supposed to be Injun sign?" Duffin inquired.

"What the sheriff means," Dusty put in, "is are we sure, seeing as how dark it was last night, that they were Indians jumped us."

Catching Dusty's glance and reading it right, the Kid gave a shrug. "They sure didn't act like Injuns."

The men had to be content with that. Although Pilsen and Bennet expected the Texans to verify their belief that Indians lay behind the trouble, Dusty and the Kid failed to do so. Showing their disappointment and anger, the two settlers mounted their horses and rode away. After suggesting, demanding even, that the affair be investigated by a U.S. Marshal, Ede and Three-Feathers rode off in the other direction. After watching the two factions depart, the sheriff swung towards Dusty.

"Just what in hell's the game, Cap'n?" he asked grimly.

"That's what I don't know," Dusty admitted. "This whole mess cuts deeper all the time. But they *were* Indians who hit at us last night."

"Then why——"

"I'm damned if I know why," Dusty interrupted. "Except that I never like to tip my hand until I've seen the rest of the cards."

"But you said——" the sheriff spluttered.

"Best listen Dusty out, Sheriff," the Kid put in. "He mostly come out with good sense, even if you don't understand it."

"Try me with some then, Cap'n," growled Duffin.

"Like I said; last night a bunch of Indians jumped us," Dusty explained. "Indians dressed in town clothes and wearing shoes, but Indians for all that. What I want to know is why they jumped us; if they turned loose the stock, bust that dam and fired the barn—and why they did it."

"It don't make sense," Duffin stated. "They know that'd make trouble for them from the settlers."

"Except that in the other cases there's no real proof that Indians did anything," Dusty pointed out. "What'd happen if the settlers got out of hand and started jumping the reservation?"

"There'd likely be a big investigation to find out why."

"And what would be found? That a few accidents happened in a storm, with no proof that they were made happen. You know that back East there's a strong political faction who'll always listen to the Indians' version first."

"Sure do, Cap'n," agreed Duffin. "That same bunch who wanted all the whites moved out of the Nations and this trail strip closed down. But this's beyond me, that's for sure."

"And me," Dusty said. "There's one thing, Sheriff. We came to tell you that Belle Starr was murdered last night."

The words brought a shocked curse to Duffin's lips as he stared at Dusty.

"Who——" Duffin began.

"We don't know. She sent word to us at Mulrooney to

come down here fast. On the way in, we found her. She'd been cut down from behind with a ten gauge."

"Lord!" Duffin gasped.

"I want you to deputize Lon, Mark and me," Dusty went on. "We aim to stick around and find the man who killed her, so if you take us on, we'll handle it and leave you and your men free to deal with this other trouble."

Duffin only hesitated for a moment, then he nodded his head. With feelings running high in Lubbock, he figured that he might need every deputy on hand and could not spare time to search for Belle Starr's killer. The three Texans could take on the investigation and possessed the knowledge to carry it through, leaving Duffin and his regular deputies free to attend to the affairs of the county.

"You're on, Cap'n," he said. "Now let's get on over to the Starr place. You can tell me all you know on the way in."

By the time the three men reached the Starr ranch, Dusty had given the sheriff all the details. A buggy and saddled horse stood before the house, Duffin recognized his first deputy's mount and Doctor Leach's transportation. Even as he mentioned the matter, Duffin saw Bessy Kissel, the elder daughter, coming from the house in something of a hurry.

"Cap'n Fog!" the girl gasped. "You'd best go into the house."

"What is it?" asked Dusty, swinging from his saddle.

"It—It's your friend."

Dusty and the Kid left their horses fast, letting the reins trail as they headed towards the house. On entering, they made for the sitting-room on the girl's heels and halted just inside the door. Mark sat at the table, rigid, unmoving, his face set in an expression of horror and distress that far exceeded his first grief.

"What is it, *amigo?*" the Kid asked, halting at Mark's

side. Slowly Mark turned his tortured eyes to his friend's and they read the hell the blond giant suffered in their depths.

"It—It's Belle!" he said, his voice a low, agonized moan. "The doctor——"

"Well?" Dusty prompted.

"He said—Belle—— He said she was carrying a child."

"My God!" Dusty breathed. "Stay with him, Lon."

Turning, Dusty left the room, closing the door behind him. He found that Bessie had fetched her mother from upstairs and the woman's face showed concern.

"What'd the doctor tell Mark?" she asked, coming forward. "I thought Mark was getting over it. He started asking questions, then the doctor called him over and said something."

"Mark didn't harm the doctor?" asked Dusty.

"No," Mrs. Kissel answered, sounding puzzled. "I thought he'd collapse when the doctor spoke to him. He just reeled, his face like death, and flopped into the chair. He's never moved since."

"Where's the doctor now?" Dusty growled.

"That's him coming."

Instead of a doddering old-timer who might let something slip by accident, Dusty found Doc Leach to be a stocky, middle-sized young man. Contrition showed on the doctor's face as he came forward.

"You'll be Captain Fog," Leach said. "Lord! What a damned fool I was. Only I thought—I never realized——"

"No," Dusty said bitterly. "You couldn't have known."

He might have said more, but common sense held back the angry words. From Leach's expression Dusty knew the doctor told the truth. Unintentional though the slip had been, Dusty guessed how the news must have struck Mark, coming as it did on top of the shock of finding Belle dead. Yet the doctor could not be blamed for failing to know of the girl's relationship with the blond giant.

"I—I thought he was just a friend, and one with enough lawman savvy to hunt down the killer," Leach went on. "He started asking me about Belle's friends—I never realized——"

"I know that, Doctor," Dusty said gently.

"I'll go and tend to Winnie Starr, Doc," Mrs. Kissel remarked, showing surprising tact.

After the woman had passed beyond ear-shot, Dusty asked, "How long had she been carrying the child, Doctor?"

"I couldn't say without opening her up. And even then wouldn't know to a month or so. I'd say not longer than four months or less than two."

"Huh, huh!" Dusty grunted. "One thing, Doctor."

"Yes?"

"Don't mention this to anybody. Let her carry it to the grave."

"She was my friend too, mine and my wife's," Leach stated. "God! If I'd only known how things stood between——"

"Drop it, Doc!" Dusty ordered. "You couldn't know. Leave Mark to me. You take care of—everything."

"I'll take care of it," Leach promised. "I'm taking the Starrs into town for a few days."

At that moment Duffin entered. "Where's Blue Duck, Doc?" he asked.

"That's strange, I've not seen him since I arrived," Leach answered.

"Who might Blue Duck be?" Dusty inquired.

"The Starrs' hired man," Duffin explained. "Young Injun, but he's been on the ranch more than the reservation all his grown life."

"Only he's not here today," Dusty said, and his eyes swung to Leach. "Reckon I could talk to Pop Starr?"

"I reckon so," Leach replied. "He seems to be shaking himself together."

"Does he know about——" Dusty began and let the words trail off.

"No. At least I haven't told him."

"I'll see him then. Coming, Sheriff?"

"Figure you can handle it without my help, Cap'n," Duffin answered. "I'll leave it in your hands. I'd best get back to town as soon as I can." He dipped his right hand into his pocket and took something out. "Saw Stalky and borrowed his badge for you. Put it on, and you're fully deputized as of now."

"Thanks, Bill," Dusty said, taking the deputy's badge and pinning it to his calf-skin vest. "I'll never forget your help."

"Just don't forget you're wearing one of my badges when you catch the man who killed Belle," Duffin warned quietly.

"I'll mind that," Dusty promised.

"Lord help you, whoever you are," breathed Duffin as Dusty turned and walked back into the house. "Those three boys'll never leave off until they've nailed your stinking hide to the door."

In the hall Dusty found the Kid waiting. "I gave Mark a bottle of whisky," the dark youngster said.

"That's no answer for him," Dusty replied.

"What is the answer?" growled the Kid.

"I'm damned if I know, Lon. I'm just damned if I know."

With that Dusty walked from the hall and to the kitchen where he found the two Kissel girls. On asking where Belle's father could be found, Dusty was told to go out on the back porch. Followed by the Kid, Dusty walked out of the kitchen and through the rear door. Neither of them looked forward to the interview they must have with the grieving man, but knew it must be done.

In his prime Jack Starr had been a big, burly, hearty man. Some traces of the man's mighty physique showed, although he seemed to have shrunk into himself in his grief. A lined, ashy-pale face turned to the two Texans as they came on to the porch and walked towards Starr.

"There's not much a man can say at a time like this, Jack," Dusty said.

"Get whoever killed her, Cap'n Fog," Starr replied.

"We aim to," Dusty answered. "Only we need some help. Reckon you can answer some questions for us?"

Slowly Starr's frame began to bulk out and determination came to his lined, grief-marked face. Straightening in the chair he looked up at Dusty and nodded his head.

"I reckon I can, Cap'n. What do you want to know?"

"Who'd have reason to kill Belle?"

"Nobody I know of."

"How about folks she———" Dusty paused, not sure how to go on.

"Took for some of their money?" Starr finished for him. "I know what my gal did on her trips, Cap'n. She went out first to help get money to keep this place going. We needed money bad and she went to answer an advertisement in a newspaper. Only the feller who put it there wanted more than just a teacher for his daughter. Belle took him for a thousand dollars on some dodge she'd heard the boys talk about. After that, well she got a liking for it. Only I don't reckon she ever gave anybody she took cause to want her dead."

"Where'd she go last?" the Kid inquired.

"She never told us where she went, or what she did while she was away," Starr replied. "Came back with twenty thousand dollars near enough."

A low whistle left Dusty's lips. While he knew little or nothing of Belle's criminal activity, he figured that the amount must be well above what she usually made on her swindles. Maybe the man who lost such a large sum had not taken the deficit lightly and sought the girl out with revenge in mind. However, that did not explain how Belle came to be riding through a storm, or how the killer knew where to lay in wait for her.

"You've no idea where she went last then?"

"None at all," admitted Starr.

Maybe Mark could help, Dusty thought. The blond giant met up with Belle in Santa Fe, perhaps he could suggest where she went from there. However, Dusty wanted to learn all he could from Belle's father before trying elsewhere.

"How long is it since Belle came back?"

"About six weeks."

"And what she been doing since then?"

"Stayed around the place, help Maw, or me. She seemed quieter than usual, when she talked, it was about Mark Counter. She acted like she was in love with him. Then she started to meeting that dude from the Injun College."

"Ede?" asked Dusty.

"That's him. Met up with him at a dance in town and started seeing him regular. A mite too regular to my way of thinking. Just laughed when I asked her about it. Told me not to worry, there wasn't anything likely to come of it."

"Why'd she go out last night?"

"We were all set to go to bed, and she went out to check that everything was all right. Been gone maybe ten minutes when she came back in a hurry, said she has to go over to Poppy Grayne's place as Poppy'd took ill. Hell, she'd been fetched out that way afore so we never thought——"

"Easy," Dusty said gently as Starr's words died off and the man clenched his big hands. "Did she say who brought the message?"

"No. We figured it was Poppy's eldest boy. Belle was in a rush and we didn't waste time asking questions."

"Ride over to the Grayne place and ask if they sent, Lon," Dusty ordered, "I'll go see Ede at the reservation." Then a thought struck him and he turned his attention back to Starr. "Say, where's Blue Duck?"

"Huh?" grunted the rancher. "Hell, I haven't seen him for a week. In fact ever since he started to go to that damned Injun College he's been no use as a hand. Never here when he's wanted. I figured he ought to have a chance at book-learning, so I let him go."

"How'd he and Belle get on?"

"Like brother'n sister. We treated him like one of the family."

"Did Belle see much of him after she came back from her last trip?"

"It was him that introduced her to Ede. But Blue Duck doesn't know anything about Belle's——"

Starr came to a halt, unable to mention the next word. Thoughts surged into Dusty's head, pouring through in a torrent. Yet none came to anything, nor would they until he asked more questions. Some of the answers he needed lay at the Indian reservation, in the school for grown-up males known as the College. Dusty decided that the sooner he learned those answers, the nearer he might be to finding Belle's killer.

"We'll tend to things here for you," he promised Starr.

"Thanks, Cap'n. I aim to keep Maw in town for a few days until she's over the shock. Reckon you'll get whoever did it?"

"We surely aim to try."

"When you get him," Starr said grimly. "Let me have the bastard—alive."

CHAPTER EIGHT

Couch's Last Mistake

"Those carbines were WHAT!" Dusty bellowed, standing in the Indian Agency's main office and glaring across the desk at a worried-looking Tiltman.

"I'm sorry, Captain Fog," the agent answered. "After you rode out, I left the office to make arrangements to have the door fixed. While I was gone, Sergeant Buffalo, one of my policemen, came in, saw the carbines and put them into the armory with our weapons."

While riding from the Starr place to the reservation, Dusty suddenly realized how information about the carbines could be obtained. A telegraph message to the National Armory at Springfield, Illinois, listing the five carbines' serial numbers, would establish whether they had been issued to a cavalry unit from which they might have fallen into hostile Indian hands, or if they went to the Indian Affairs Bureau to arm reservation policemen. So, before visiting Ede to ask questions about the man's friendship with Belle Starr, Dusty called in on Tiltman—and discovered that the five guns had been taken into the armory of the Agency, which held fifty all but identical weapons.

"Where's Buffalo now?" Dusty growled.

"He rode out soon after I saw him and I don't know which way he went."

"Do you let him keep a key to the armory?"

"Why not?" Tiltman yelped indignantly. "He's a sergeant of reservation police. We have to show our men that we trust them."

"I reckon you do," Dusty agreed. "How about your records of arms issued to the Agency?"

"I'm afraid they're not very accurate. It's difficult keeping track on the coming and going of the carbines as none of the reservation police can read or write. I do the best I can, but there's so much to do."

"Can I take a look in the armory?"

"Of course. Come with me."

Dusty followed Tiltman into the room at the rear of the office, and looked at the five racks on which stood the spare carbines. Going to the nearest rack, Dusty lifted out one of the guns noticing that it and all the others in the room had tack-decorated butts. This did not surprise Dusty for he had never seen an Indian firearm which did not carry medicine patterns in its woodwork. Opening the carbine's breech, Dusty placed his thumb into the cavity and held the weapon so he could look down the barrel. In the light reflected by his thumb-nail Dusty saw what might be the answer to his problem.

"This carbine's been fired and not cleaned," he said. "Which we didn't take time to clean the five we brought in."

"I don't think it's one you want," Tiltman replied. "That first rack had ten carbines on it when I looked in this morning."

There was only ten of the little guns on the rack, or would be when Dusty returned the one he held. Slapping shut the trapdoor breech. Dusty replaced the carbine. He went to the next rack and took a gun at random, on a check it proved to be clean. However, the next two Dusty examined showed to have been fired and not cleaned. So did ten more on the second and third rack and the proportion remained constant as he examined the other two racks. All Dusty proved was that Tiltman's police did not take very good care of the weapons in the armory. He could not even start to guess at which were the five carbines he and the Kid brought in with them.

"I'm not a military man, Captain," Tiltman apologized when Dusty showed him the condition of the weapons. "Not knowing about firearms, I left the running of the armory to Sergeant Couch."

Dusty was a fair judge of character and guessed the Agent told the truth. An expression of worry showed plain on Tiltman's face, but Dusty put it down to the man being afraid of what a report of his failings might do to his career.

"Was I you, I'd get all the guns cleaned," Dusty suggested. "And I'd start keeping a careful record of their serial numbers. Do you know how much ammunition you have on hand?"

"Not an accurate idea. You know how these Indians are. They fire off a few shots and come in to replenish. It's all but impossible to keep an accurate record."

"Reckon you'd best try. It's none of my affair, but if trouble comes there might be questions asked about how much ammunition you have on hand and where the rest went. Where do I find Ede?"

"At the Indian College," Tiltman replied. "It's about a mile from here, along that trail which leads into the woods. The College lies behind the trees, you can't see it from here." Then a thought struck the Agent. "You don't think Mr. Ede knows anything about the raid on your camp?"

"I just want to see him on another matter. Say, you could try to sort out those five carbines. It'd help you if we can prove the guns we brought in weren't issued to your reservation police."

"It might at that." Tiltman agreed, eager to clear his men of the suspicions he knew would be flashing around town. "I'll see what I can do."

Taking his horse, Dusty rode along the west-bound trail

which led into a section of fairly thick wooded country. Although the trail he followed had been well used and was wide enough for a Conestoga wagon to travel along, the bush came down fairly thickly on either side and effectively hid the College from view. Dusty rode in a relaxed manner but he kept his eyes open and ears working. His eyes flickered from side to side in swift glances that missed little. Although his hands held the reins, they were ready to stab across to the waiting guns. Yet for all his precautions, Dusty saw nothing to disturb him on the half-mile ride through the wooded country, and came into view of the Indian College without seeing any sign of human beings.

Despite its high-sounding name, the Indian College consisted of nothing more than a line of half-a-dozen large one floor cabins and a few smaller buildings. Only four horses moved in the large corral, good quality mounts, not the usual under-fed, wiry animals used by the Indians. Apparently classes had ended for the day, which did not surprise Dusty as the time was almost six o'clock, and the pupils gone home. However, smoke rose from the chimney of one of the smaller buildings, so Dusty rode in its direction.

Studying the peaceful, harmless scene before him, Dusty wondered why he felt so uneasy. True, the attackers dressed in town clothing, but many Indians in Oklahoma worked in the white men's towns and dressed accordingly. Springfield carbines were not in such short supply that obtaining them would be all but impossible. If it came to a point, many such guns probably lay around the reservations in Indian hands. Maybe Dusty allowed his dislike for Mrs. Ford to cloud his judgement. One thing a lawman must always do, keep an open mind while making an investigation. With that thought in mind, Dusty swung from his saddle outside the small cabin.

"What do you want?" asked Three-Feathers, opening the door in answer to Dusty's knock.

"I'd like to see Mr. Ede," Dusty replied.

"Why?"

"If you'd do, I wouldn't be asking for him."

"Maybe David Ede doesn't want to see you," Three-Feathers growled.

A bleak grin twisted Dusty's lips. "We can do it hard or easy, *hombre*. But whichever way it goes, I aim to see Ede right now."

For a moment Three-Feathers hesitated, studying Dusty—one point the Indian missed being Dusty's badge, for the Texan had concealed it before visiting Tiltman to avoid having to answer unnecessary questions—and thinking of Couch's fate when trying to rough-handle the small man. Noting the grim determination on Dusty's face, Three-Feathers gave a shrug and looked back into the cabin.

"A visitor, David," he said.

Ede appeared at the door, scowling when he saw the caller. "What do you want here?" he asked sullenly.

"To talk with you."

"I thought you'd decided that Indians weren't to blame for the attack on your camp," Ede said, still sullen.

"All I said was that there were things about the raid that didn't look like Indian work," Dusty countered.

"You couldn't prove anything without the bodies of your attackers," Three-Feathers put in. "It was a pity you didn't examine them in daylight."

"We *did* examine them in daylight."

"Then you'd know——" Ede began.

"Yes, Mr. Ede," agreed Dusty. "We know that Indians attacked us."

"Then why did you——" Three-Feathers growled.

"Say what we did? To stop trouble bursting out. I wouldn't have done the settlers any good to have it said they invaded the reservation and made trouble."

"After the way you handled it, nobody will believe that

Indians attacked you," Ede pointed out, satisfaction showing in his voice.

"Maybe not. Only I intend to let the Kid go cut for sign. You can't move five bodies without leaving plenty of tracks, and the Ysabel Kid's a boy who can follow sign. He'll find where the bodies went, then we'll have our proof."

"You're a smarter man than we thought, Captain Fog," the Indian said.

"Most folks are," Dusty answered.

"You didn't just come here to tell us that," Ede put in.

"No. I came to see you about Belle Starr."

"Belle Starr?" repeated Ede. "What about her?"

"How well do you know her?"

"That's my business!" The Easterner yelped. "You've no right to——"

The words trailed off as Dusty took out the deputy's badge and showed it to the two young men. Although Ede stared down at the badge. Three-Feathers kept his eyes on Dusty's face and his mouth shut.

"Sheriff Duffin deputized me," Dusty announced.

"Why?" Ede asked, his voice hoarse.

"Needed extra men. So he took me on and told me to find the man who murdered Belle Starr."

Dusty had thought of how he would handle the questioning and decided a blunt approach might best serve him when dealing with Ede. Certainly the young man seemed to be shocked by the words. For a moment fear and panic warred on Ede's face.

"All right, come in," he said, and stood aside.

"I'll leave you to talk in private," Three-Feathers remarked. "It would be best for all concerned."

Dusty formed the opinion that the words had been designed to lull Ede's concern. Once again the old instinct began to nag at Dusty, warning him of danger in the air.

Yet he could see nothing suspicious, unless he counted Three-Feathers's willingness to help. Yet the Indian made a good point. If Ede refused to answer questions, folks would regard it as an admission of guilty knowledge. Maybe Three-Feathers acted only in his friend's best interest.

After Dusty entered the room, Three-Feathers walked out and closed the door. Alert as ever, Dusty saw the Indian walk by one of the side windows and away from the building. When Dusty turned his attention to Ede, he found that the other appeared to be composed and calm.

"What do you want to know?" Ede asked.

"How well did you know Belle?"

"Not too w——Oh, all right, I knew her pretty well. We met regularly——"

"Did you make love?"

"No! It was just that—well, she could talk about things in an interesting manner. Can you imagine what it's like trying to make decent conversation with these red s——, with the students here?"

"Not easy, I reckon," Dusty admitted.

"That's all there was to it. Just friendship. She had knowledge of the world and I liked her company."

"And you never tried to take it further?"

"I—I'd have liked to, but never did."

"When did you see her last?"

"About a week ago."

"Did you quarrel?"

"No. We never quarrelled.. I didn't kill her."

"Why'd you act so nervous when I started asking about Belle?" Dusty asked.

Once more the worry came to Ede's face. It held for a moment, then cleared. "Because you're a southerner and everybody knows how they regard us Republicans."

"You'd best tie that for me," Dusty drawled.

"I—I thought that you might try to incriminate me."

"Now why'd I do that?"

"Some southerners would go to any extreme to smear a Republican."

"Huh huh!" grunted Dusty. "Where were you last night?"

"At Deacon Forster's house, all night. I went there to see him and the storm prevented me from coming home until this morning. You can check on it."

"I know I can. Say, do you have any guns around the place?"

"I——Yes, a few rifles. The Agency don't pay us so well that we can live without shooting meat. Not that I hunt for sport."

"Do you have a double-barrelled ten gauge?"

"No!" snapped Ede, but he flickered a nervous glance at the cupboard on the left side of the small dining-room.

Dusty reached the cupboard in three strides and jerked open the door. A few coats, a couple of fish and some hats hung inside; and leaning against the wall, their levers showing, were three single-barrelled rifles.

"I told you so," Ede said as Dusty shut the door. Once more the small Texan caught a note of relief in the man's voice.

"All right, Mr. Ede," he said. "Call your *amigo* in so that I can ask him where he was last night."

"With me," Ede answered.

"I'd still like to ask him myself," Dusty drawled.

Giving a shrug, Ede went to the front door, opened and called Three-Feathers' name. A minute passed, then the Indian walked into the cabin, glancing at Ede, then giving Dusty his full attention. Three-Feathers answered Dusty's questions without hesitation and offered the same alibi for his whereabouts the previous night as had Ede. Not even by a flicker of an eye-lid did Three-Feathers show any concern when Dusty asked about ownership of a double-barrel shotgun.

"Search if you wish," the Indian said, waving a hand towards the cupboard door. "There are three lever action rifles inside——"

"I've already seen them," Dusty replied. "Thanks for giving me your time."

With that Dusty turned and walked out of the cabin, leaving the door open. Even as he swung into his saddle, Dusty heard the door slam, but he did not look back. Instead he rode towards the wooded country, knowing the two young men watched him go and sure he had started them thinking.

Holding his horse to an easy walk, Dusty started to think about his visit to the Indian College. If Ede's account of his whereabouts the previous night proved to be true, and Dusty did not doubt that it would, the young man could not be Belle's killer. Which caused Dusty to wonder why Ede showed such agitation on hearing what brought the small Texan to the College. Of course, Ede's suggestion that he thought Dusty might be trying to establish a false charge merely to smear a political opposite could have accounted for the agitation. Smearing political rivals had always been a prime tactic of Ede's kind and his type of mentality always wanted to reduce everybody to its own level.

A splash of dark blue on the right of the trail caught the corner of Dusty's eye. As his brain screamed a warning that no such color should be present, a gun roared and flame ripped from the offending color patch. Even as a bullet fanned the air by his face, Dusty pitched sideways off his horse. He went to the left, drawing both guns as he fell and landed rolling. Letting the right-hand Colt drop on to the trail, Dusty continued to roll until his body was partially hidden under a bush at the side of the trail. Once there, he concealed the left hand with its lethal load and lay still waiting for his assailant to come up and inspect his marksmanship. Once that happened, Dusty hoped to take a living prisoner who might be induced to answer questions.

Moving cautiously and silently, Couch came through the bushes and towards the trail. His eyes studied the open ground and he gave a low curse as he discovered that Dusty's roll took the small Texan out of sight. However, that bone-handled Colt lying in the trail told a story to Couch's way of thinking. A gunfighter like Dusty Fog would never drop his weapon unless so badly injured that he could no longer hold it. Not that Couch intended to take any chances. Already he cursed himself for the stupid mistakes he made in setting up his ambush. His fear of the Rio Hondo gun wizard's skill caused him to hide further from the track than was wise; and a newly broken and set nose did not make for accurate long range shooting with a handgun. While he appeared to have scored a lucky hit, Couch aimed to make *real* sure of the small Texan before going within grabbing distance of the other's hands.

Halting at the side of the trail, Couch looked across, seeing Dusty as the Texan lay partially concealed under the bush at the other side. Up came the long-barrelled Cavalry Colt and roared, kicking with the recoil. Dusty sensed rather than saw his danger and tried to roll into the open where he could bring his left-hand gun into line. A slight hollow had formed under the bush and it held Dusty for a moment. Something red hot seared across Dusty's back, a burning touch he knew all too well. With a desperate heave, Dusty twisted his body out of the hollow, rolling towards where Couch stood thumb-cocking his Colt as its barrel weight brought it into line again. There would be no time to complete the roll and land on his stomach, but Dusty had learned to handle his guns from any position. Still on his back, he lined the Colt and fired, shooting the only way he dare under the circumstances. Caught in the head by a .45 bullet, Couch rocked over backwards, his gun firing harmlessly into the trail's dirt as it fell from a lifeless hand.

Slowly Dusty came to his feet. He bent down, retrieved the right-hand Colt and returned it to its holster. Then he walked towards Couch who had made his last mistake when he took chances with Dusty Fog.

Feet thudded on the trail, approaching rapidly. Three-Feathers burst into sight of the ambush ground and came skidding to a halt, the rifle in his hands held down before him as Dusty's Colt turned in his direction.

"Just hold it right there," Dusty ordered.

"I heard the shots and came——" Three-Feathers began, then stopped and stared at the shape on the trail. "That's Couch!"

"Looks that way," Dusty agreed. "He tried to kill me—twice."

"You must admit that he had good cause to hate you."

"Likely."

"I suppose he saw you coming this way and laid in wait for you as you rode back," Three-Feathers suggested.

"Looks that way," Dusty agreed. "Pick up his Colt and come with me to the Agency."

"Why?"

"Because I aim to have it on record what happened here. Just in case anybody wants to make something different about it later."

"Do you think anybody would try to make out that you did not kill Couch in self-defense?" asked the Indian.

"I don't know," Dusty replied. "But I sure as hell don't aim to give them the chance."

CHAPTER NINE

The Coming of Calamity

"He's still the same," Dusty said, coming from the house and walking to where the Kid stood saddling the big white stallion.

It was three days after Belle Starr's death and Mark still remained sunk into the state of shock which followed his discovery that she carried an unborn child. The blond giant had hardly spoken or eaten in three days and spent all his time restlessly prowling the house or sitting in the main room staring blankly at the piano which Belle must often have played.

"It might be best to take him away from here for a spell," the Kid suggested. "Get him out of sight of things that remind him of her."

"I thought of it, Lon," Dusty admitted. "Only it wouldn't work. He's got to lick this thing here, or he's finished."

"I wish to the Lord he'd get drunk, or smash something," the Kid growled. "He's never been like this afore."

"He's never had such a shock before either, Lon," Dusty pointed out. "Reckon you can find Blue Duck?"

"I'm going to make a stab at it."

Leaving Mark in Mrs. Kissel's care, Dusty and the Kid had spent hours in their saddles, trying to learn something to aid them in their search for Belle's killer. Sheriff Duffin came out regularly with reports on the other affair. Using his senior deputy's skill as a tracker, Duffin tried to find the bodies of Dusty's attackers, but the sign ended in a river and could not be found again. Feelings had begun to simmer down in Lubbock when no further trouble happened. Dusty's killing of Couch had been cleared up satisfactorily, with Tiltman listening to the Texan's evidence and checking the weapons involved. Showing a surprising grasp of the situation, Tiltman stated that Couch must have fired twice at Dusty before the small Texan shot back, for no man could get off two shots from a single-action revolver, *after* being hit in the head with a .45 bullet. Three-Feathers' evidence that he arrived on the scene straight after the shooting, and too soon for Dusty to have changed loads in the revolvers, strengthened Dusty's case, as did the messy, painful, but neither deep nor dangerous bullet nick across the Texan's back.

Dusty and the Kid had learned little in their search for Belle's killer. However, their questions established two things: first, Mrs. Ford never came to Lubbock and as far as anybody knew had never met Belle—although rumor stated that the woman's interest in Ede was more than professional; second, that Blue Duck considered himself to be Belle's lover and told a friend he aimed to marry the girl. Armed with that knowledge, Dusty tried to locate Blue Duck, but neither the Agency nor the College could offer any hint of where the Indian might be.

"You've been trying the wrong places," the Kid stated as they rode away from the Agency after their abortive attempt to locate the missing Blue Duck. "I'll try it my way."

"Go to it," Dusty answered, glancing at the sky. "Only it looks like a storm coming up."

That had been the previous evening and the storm materialized just after they reached the Starr place. For almost four hours rain came down heavily, although neither thunder nor lightning added force to the fury of the falling water. Now it was daylight and the Kid prepared to ride out. He would be taking along two spare horses; animals trained by Starr to work as a relay team, following the ridden mount and ready to take its place as it tired. Just where he meant to go and what he aimed to do the Kid had not said, nor did Dusty ask. When the Kid dealt with Indians, he often used lessons learned from his grandfather's lodge brothers and given in confidence under a lodge oath of silence. Dusty never asked the Kid to break his oath and allowed the other a free hand to handle the affair as he saw fit.

"When're you likely to be back?" Dusty asked.

"Maybe two, three day's time."

"Which means you don't know for sure."

"You might say that," agreed the Kid. "See you, Dusty. Take care of Mark."

Swinging astride the white, the Kid caught up his relay's lead ropes and rode off in a north-westerly direction. Dusty watched his friend fade off into the distance and then went to make a start on the routine chores of the ranch. An hour passed and Dusty halted in his work in the barn, listening to the sound of approaching hooves. Laying aside the pitchfork, Dusty scooped a Colt from his gunbelt in passing where it hung on a peg. Only one horse approached, but precautions cost nothing even though they helped keep a man alive.

"You been having fuss too, Cap'n?" asked Bill Duffin's senior deputy, halting his horse and looking at the Colt.

"Should we have been?" Dusty countered and thrust the revolver into his waistband.

"Bennet had him fifty head of whitefaces held in a basin ready for shipping. Only last night in the rain they up and went. Ran over a coulee and he lost maybe fifteen prime steers. Rain made the Guthrie stage late, it was coming through Eagle Valley in the storm and damned near got buried under a rock fall."

"Anything else?"

"Land-sakes, Cap'n, ain't that enough?" yelped Stalky. "Leastways, that's all we heard about. And guess what folks're saying?"

"That the Indians are responsible," Dusty answered.

"You been peeking," objected Stalky.

"What's the sheriff want me to do?"

"Nothing. Just figured you'd be interested and might have some ideas. He says for you to stay on working at finding Belle's killer. Bill figures to keep close to town in case anybody starts getting fool notions."

"Has he seen the places where the trouble happened?"

"Nope. I went out. No sign, it's all been washed out by the rain. Mind you, there's been rock falls in that valley afore. Stage line wouldn't go through the bottom only it'd add five or six miles to the trip to go around."

"And the herd?" asked Dusty.

"Now there I'd say it was a mite peculiar. They'd been bedded down on good grass and decent water. Been sheltered from the rain too. Which same worried me."

"And me, Stalky. Whitefaces don't spook easy and don't take to night moving unless they're pushed hard."

"Yeah," said Stalky dryly. "Only this bunch did. I cut around and couldn't find a blessed trace to show what spooked 'em. Best be heading back now."

"You have time for a cup of coffee?"

"Like to, but things were a mite hot in town."

"Tell Bill I'll be here all day if he needs me."

"Thanks, Cap'n. It'll help cool folks down happen they know *you're* fixing to back us should they cut out all wild and rambunctious."

A puzzled Dusty returned to his work after Stalky rode

away. He did not fail to grasp one significant point; that on the two rainless nights nothing happened. While finishing the haying of the stalls, Dusty tried to work out what lay behind the mysterious incidents and formed several theories all of which would cover at least some of the aspects of the business.

Dusty was still thinking over the problem when he finished his work in the barn. While strapping on his gunbelt, he heard the sound of hooves. Walking to the door, Dusty looked out and did not know whether to feel pleased or sorry when he recognised the new arrival.

A battered U.S. cavalry kepi perched jauntily on a mop of shortish, curly red hair which framed a freckled, pretty, though not out-and-out beautiful face. Normally the kissable lips wore a warm, merry grin, but were now twisted into sober lines which matched the tired lines of the rest of the face. A silk bandana knotted around a tan-throat trailed its ends down over a shirt which, like the levis pants, looked to have been bought a size too small and shrunk in the wash. As always, the shirt's neck was open far enough to show the valley between the rich, full breasts which strained against the material. The waist slimmed down without artificial aids and the levis clung tight to full, shapely hips that hinted at eye-catching legs below them. Butt forward in a fast-draw holster at the right side of a well-made gunbelt hung an ivory-handled Navy Colt which had been rechambered to fire metal cartridges; and a soiled bull whip thrust into the left side of the rider's waistband. Dusty knew neither gun nor whip was a mere affectation.

The girl rode a fine buckskin gelding, sitting slouched in her Cheyenne Roll saddle as if tired. From the look of it, the buckskin had covered some miles in a hurry. Yet the girl raised her hand and managed to smile as she saw the small Texan walking towards her.

"Howdy, Dusty," she said, her voice as tired as her general appearance. "I heard about it up in Newton two days back. Come right down. Didn't know you boys were here."

Jumping forward, Dusty helped the girl down. To reach the Starr place from Newton, Kansas, in so short a time meant that she could have spent little time out of the saddle.

"Pleased to see you, Calam," Dusty answered. "Come on to the house."

"Thanks. How's Mark taking it?"

"Bad, girl, real bad."

Just how bad Calamity Jane began to realize as she entered the house and looked through the open door of the sitting-room. Mark sat slumped at the table, an open bottle of whisky and a glass before him and a look she could hardly believe she saw on his face. Although Calamity stood for a moment, Mark did not even give a sign that he knew of her presence. Gently Dusty took the girl's arm and led her into the kitchen. Mrs. Kissel stood at the stove and turned as she heard Dusty and the girl enter. A hint of disapproval creased the woman's face as she looked Calamity up and down, with special emphasis on the front of the girl's shirt.

Before Calamity could make the comment Dusty expected to hear, he stepped forward and looked straight at Mrs. Kissel.

"This's Calamity Jane, Mrs. Kissel," he said, then paused before going on in a warning tone, "She and Belle were friends."

Only for a moment did the disapproval hold. There was much about Calamity's dress and behavior that a woman like Mrs. Kissel took exception to, but the rancher's wife also acknowledged that the girl possessed many sterling qualities. There was another very important point in Calamity's favor where Mrs. Kissel was concerned.

"Belle often spoke of you, Calamity," she said, "and always as a friend."

"Give Herb a shout, ma'am, ask him to tend to Calam's horse."

"As soon as I've poured Calamity a cup of coffee and put food before her. The poor girl looks gaunt with hunger."

Not until Calamity had eaten and drunk a cup of coffee did Mrs. Kissel leave the kitchen. Once alone with Dusty, Calamity got straight down to business.

"Tell me all about it," she said.

Simply and without holding back a single fact, even that Belle carried an unborn child, Dusty told Calamity all he knew. Nothing he had done seemed to shake Mark out of his state of shock, perhaps Calamity might be able to strike the note and force the blond giant to his senses. Looking at the girl, Dusty thought of what he knew about her.

In her own right Calamity Jane was every bit as much a legend as Dusty Fog, Mark Counter, the Ysabel Kid or any of the well-known westerners. Many tales had been told of her prowess at driving a six-horse Conestoga wagon; handling a bull whip as inducement to effort and weapon; skill with firearms; and ability in an all-in, hand-scalping barroom catfight. Most of the stories had some basis of truth and Dusty admired Calamity for her courage, loyalty to her friends and general love of life. Calamity lived every day to the full—and was much like Belle Starr in that respect.

More important, Calamity and Mark had been real close, in fact the girl knew the blond giant almost as intimately as Belle had; although Calamity, always a realist, knew nothing would ever develop from her nights with the big Texan, or wanted it to. Maybe Calamity could strike the right note, sink through Mark's shock and get his mind working again.

"Poor Mark," she said quietly. "Can I go see him, Dusty?"

"I hoped you would," he replied.

"Let me handle it my way," she went on, her mouth twisting into grim, bitter lines. "No matter what you hear, don't come near."

Dusty studied Calamity's face for a good minute before he nodded. "It's your deal, Calam. Play them how you want."

Sucking in a deep breath, Calamity shoved back her chair and rose. Without another word, looking as if she wanted Dusty to stop her and was leaving hurriedly before he could, she walked from the kitchen. Dusty took out tobacco and papers, but somehow he could not seem to make a cigarette. Angrily he thrust the smoke-material away and sat drumming his fingers on the table top.

Suddenly something crashed into the wall and, from the sound of it, the sitting-room table went over. Mrs. Kissel dashed into the kitchen, her face pale, but Dusty sprang forward and held the door into the hall so she could not open it.

"Leave it, Mrs. Kissel," he said. "At least for a few more minutes."

Calamity walked into the sitting-room, closing its door behind her. A feeling of shock hit her as she came to Mark's side and saw the ravages grief left on his face. Although he looked up, Mark did not seem to know Calamity and she drew a deep breath, taking time to gather her courage for what she knew she must do.

"Hello, Mark," she greeted gently.

Slowly Mark's eyes lifted to the girl's and recognition crept into his face. "Calam!" he said, his voice dull and toneless.

"What——? How——?"

"She was my friend, Mark," the girl told him quietly.

"Belle's dead, Calam," Mark droned on, clearly not hav-

ing even noticed she spoke to him. He sounded as if he
tried to convince himself that the words were not true.

"I know. That's why I came. To help you get the bastard
who killed her."

No result! Calamity hoped her words might shake Mark
into thought of revenge and make him start to throw off his
shock and grief. Seeing her failure, Calamity prepared to
go on with the course she planned as she entered the room.

"Belle was carrying a child, Calam. It might have been
mine."

Calamity saw her opening and only hesitated for a moment. Yet it took all her undoubted courage to force out
her next words.

"I'd say that was likely," she told Mark, looking him
squarely in the face and locking his eyes with her own.
"Belle was like me, she knew the Indian way of stopping
it before it started. So if she carried a child, it was because
she wanted to have it."

Life glowed in Mark's eyes. Cold, savage fury filled
them as he glared at Calamity and growled. "Damn you to
hell! Belle's dead——"

"I know it!" Calamity yelled back. "And it's time you
faced up to it. She's dead and you sitting here filling your
guts with whisky won't bring her back——"

Mark came to his feet, throwing the chair backwards
with such force that it crashed into the wall and shattered.
Over went the table as if it had never been there and Mark
sprang at the girl. Calamity stood without moving, even
though Mark left himself open to all kinds of attack designed
to break his hold, while the hands which had snapped the
neck of a Texas longhorn bull,* and which she had seen
raise her wagon out of a gopher hole, gripped her shoulders,

*Told in *The Man from Texas*, by J. T. Edson.

the thumbs moving towards her throat.

"Go ahead if it'll make you feel any better," she said, trying to hold her voice calm and unconcerned. "It'll be easier than going out to find her killer."

Nothing happened for what Calamity thought to be two or three hours, but in reality was only a minute. She stood still, feeling the great strength of the hands, feeling the fingers twitch and expecting at any moment to be choked at least insensible. Then slowly Mark's hands moved, sliding down her arm and drawing her to him gently.

"Calam!" he said, and at last she detected feeling in his voice. "Lord, Calam gal, did I hurt you?"

"Damn near bust both my shoulders, you big buffalo," she answered with almost a flash of the old Calamity he knew so well in her voice. "Mark—about what I said just now——"

"I know why you said it and I reckon Belle'd've wanted you to say it," he answered, then he released her and looked around, his eyes halting on the overturned table. "Did I do that?"

"You always was a mite clumsy," Calam smiled, or tried to smile through the tears which trickled down her cheeks. "Set it up again and I'll tidy up the mess. Say, do you mind that first night I met Belle?"

"Sure. I'd only met her the night before myself."

"And me the night afore that. Only I never meant anything to you, not like Belle did."

"I'm——"

"Don't apologize, Mark," Calamity interrupted. "I knew what to expect and I've only one complaint. No other feller's been the same after knowing you. But it was different with Belle. I met up with her in the Dakotas one time and we spent the night sitting making woman-talk. That gal loved you from the start—and you was the only man who ever got *that* far with her. Say, do you mind how I started to draw a moustache on that wanted poster, not knowing it was Belle with me?"

A faint smile came to Mark's lips as he thought of the first time he met Belle. That had been quite an exciting spell one way and another, for he tangled a bunch of outlaws who thought Belle could lead them to the loot of a robbery and wound up facing a bounty hunter who aimed to kill the girl and collect the price on her head.*

On the night before Mark met Belle, Calamity had been in his arms, but it was different. With Calamity it had merely been her way of thanking him for his help at unsticking her bogged-down wagon. His feelings for Calamity never went beyond respect and friendly regard for her many good qualities. Despite the nights spent together on that and other meetings, Mark tended to think of the girl as a favorite tomboy sister.

Mark had never regarded Belle as a sister. On their second meeting she saved him from a bunch of gun-wild young fools who planned to make her help them rob a stage, although he rescued her at the same time. Thinking back, Mark remembered something she said the morning after before they separated.

"I don't make a habit of this, Mark."

And she meant it, wanting him to know that she did not throw herself at every man who came along.

After that meeting, their paths crossed frequently. Mark thought back to the meetings, on the trail, while handling Ole Devil's business, and one when Belle attended the traditional Turkey Shoot held each Christmas at the OD Connected—quite a visit that, for Belle danced with Captain Murat of the Texas Rangers and gave him a tip-off which

---

*Told in *Troubled Range*, by J. T. Edson.

enabled the captain to catch a bank president who planned to depart with the bank's contents. Each meeting strengthened the feeling Mark and Belle had for each other, until the last time they talked, in a round-about way, of marriage.

"She loved you, Mark," Calamity said as Mark finished talking. "And if she carried a child, it was yours. Right or wrong she must have aimed to have something of your'n even if you didn't marry."

"I meant to marry her, was fixing to come in on the way down to ask her," Mark replied, and ran a hand over his whisker-stubbled jaw. "How long is it since———?"

"Three days. Dusty and Lon've made a start, but don't know much yet."

"Where're they now?"

"Lon's rode out. Dusty's waiting in the kitchen and likely raising a muck-sweat wondering what's happening. You go wash and shave while I tide the mess. Then we'll eat a good meal and set ourselves up for going to find Belle's killer."

Walking from the room, Mark went to the kitchen and found Dusty seated at the table while a pallid Mrs. Kissel stood at the stove cooking food. Dusty rose and faced his big friend. For almost a minute neither spoke, then Mark held out his hand. No weakling himself, Dusty winced as he felt the other's grip.

"Thanks, Dusty," Mark said.

"Good to have you back, Mark," Dusty replied. "I reckon we both owe Calam our thanks, don't you?"

On looking into the sitting-room to thank the girl, Dusty and Mark found her lying upon the settee by the window, sleeping. Dusty figured she must be worn out by the strain of the past few days and sympathized with her. He had been under quite a strain himself.

CHAPTER TEN

He Came to Warn Belle

A sharp thudding crack sound woke Calamity. For a moment she lay blinking at the rays of the sun which streamed in through the window of the room. At first Calamity could not remember where she was, then thought returned and she realized that she lay on a comfortable bed instead of the hard ground which formed her mattress most nights.

Yet Calamity could not remember climbing into bed the previous night—only it would not be the previous night. She must have dozed and either Mark or Dusty toted her upstairs where she slept undisturbed until evening.

Sitting up, Calamity threw the patchwork quilt off her and swung her feet to the floor. Her kepi, gunbelt and whip rested on a chair by the bed, her Pawnee moccasins underneath it. Nothing else had been removed, although whoever put her to bed must have unfastened her bandana a mite. Calamity gave a low groan as her muscles protested against the movement of sitting up. However, a freight driver's life hardened anybody, so the feeling ebbed out of the girl after a few minutes. Opening her shirt, she looked at the bruises left on her shoulders by Mark's thumbs.

"Whooee!" she winced. "That Mark's a tolerable tough hunk of man. Not that I need telling *that*." Glancing around the room, she could see no sign of her saddle and warbag. "I'll get one of the boys to tote it up here so's I can dig some medicine out and ease the bruising," she mused and rose to head for the washbasin.

All through Calamity's ablutions, she kept hearing the sound which woke her. With her womanly curiosity aroused, Calamity walked to the window and looked down at Dusty and Mark. The two Texans were down by the wood-pile and from all appearances Mark had been very busy. When Calamity arrived that morning a fair pile of wood waited for splitting, now only a few logs remained. Even as Calamity watched, Dusty set up a log on the big tree stump used as a chopping block and Mark swung around the double-handed axe. Down drove the axe blade, sinking into and cleaving a log most men could only have severed with a hammer and splitting-wedge. Stripped to the waist, his great muscles writhing under sweat-soaked skin, Mark stood waiting until Dusty set up another log.

"He's been doing it since dawn," said a woman's voice behind Calamity.

Turning, the girl found Mrs. Kissel at the bedroom door. Then the impact of the words hit Calamity. "Dawn?" she squealed. "But when I——Have I——?"

"You've been asleep ever since Mark carried you up yesterday afternoon," smiled Mrs. Kissel. "I don't know what you said to him, or did, but it's given Mark a new lease of life."

"It wasn't pretty, the way I did it," Calamity confessed. "But I couldn't think of another way." Then she gave a grin. "Lordy lord, I'm sure hungry."

"Then come and have breakfast—and try calling me 'Maw.' I didn't want to wake you last night, so I didn't undress you."

"Have the boys ate yet?"

"Not yet. I called them once, but they didn't come."

"Reckon you didn't call 'em the right way," Calamity grinned. "You wait until I get down and I'll give it a whirl."

"I'm always willing to learn," Mrs. Kissel replied.

On reaching the kitchen, Calamity threw open its rear door and looked out. "Come and get it right now," she yelled, and when that girl yelled chickens took to flying half a mile off, "or it goes to the hawks!"

"Reckon she'd do it, Mark?" asked Dusty in a carrying voice.

"She sure would," Mark agreed. "Got a real mean streak in her, that gal. And she's cruel to animals, which same she cooked breakfast."

"Yah!" Calamity answered, after a moment's pause while she sorted out the gist of Mark's words and came up with the answer. "The hawgs get it either way."

"Now what do your reckon she means by that?" asked Dusty.

"Don't ask me. Reckon I've time to finish splitting those last three logs?"

"Not if I know Calamity. She's like to eat our food as well as her own."

Sinking the blade of the axe deep into the top of the chopping block, Mark grinned as he listened to Calamity's pungent reply to Dusty's words. The wood chopping had offered him an outlet for his pent-up emotions and, while Belle's death still gnawed at his vitals, he now felt ready to start work on locating her killer.

On previous meetings, Calamity always struck Dusty as being a merry, courageous girl who both said and did rash things on the spur of the moment. So he hoped she would not make some remark to cause Mark further sufferings. However, throughout the meal Calamity surprised him by her display of tact and with keeping a light note in the conversation while also conveying to Mark that she sympathized with his loss.

At last, with breakfast over, Dusty knew he could not put off the business any longer and must start to ask his big *amigo* the questions which might give them an idea who killed Belle. Throwing a glance at Calamity, Dusty shoved back his chair and came to his feet.

"Let's go into the sitting-room," he suggested.

"Yes," Mark agreed in a voice as flat and emotionless as Dusty's had been. "There's things I want to know."

A silent, subdued-looking Calamity led the Texans into the sitting-room. On taking her place at the table, she reached across and laid her hand in Mark's. All the time Dusty talked, telling Mark of the little discovered so far and about the Indian trouble. Calamity sat still, her hand in Mark's grip. While listening, Calamity tried not to wince as the blond giant's fingers tightened involuntarily when some reference to Belle struck home.

"There's nothing to tie Belle to the Indian business, at least not as far as I can see," Dusty finished. "Both Ede and Three-Feathers had been in town all night and never left the house."

"Are you sure of that?" asked Mark.

"They sat up late waiting out the storm and when it didn't die went to bed there. Of course, one of them might have slipped out, but from what I saw of Deacon Forster, a man'd need to move mighty soft-footed to get by him even at night."

"But Ede looked scared when you asked about the shotgun," Calamity pointed out. "That could mean——"

"There wasn't a shotgun in the cupboard, only three lever-action rifles," Dusty objected. "And he explained why he acted nervous. His sort would think a man who didn't like them'd use any methods to get at them. That's the way they act and they reckon everybody'd do the same."

"What if Three-Feathers did sneak out?" Mark asked. "He's an Indian, even if he's been to college. Maybe he could do it."

"And ride nearly six miles through the storm, then go back and not leave a trace?" Dusty remarked. "I tell you, Mark, the Deacon's wife has a sighting eye for dirt and sin near on as good as Lon's with a rifle. She'd've seen some trace and mentioned it."

"And that doesn't tell us who got Belle out on the trail," Mark said. "She wouldn't've gone with just any chance-passing drifter."

"That's true. And it wasn't Mrs. Grayne who sent word. Lon checked."

"Those empty shotgun shells worry me, Dusty," Calamity put in. "Why'd the—the killer take time out after shooting to reload?"

"I've been puzzling on that one myself, Calam," Dusty admitted. "What do you think about it?"

"Maybe Belle was killed some other place, took there and then the killer left the shells to make you think it happened there," the girl guessed.

"And her horse?"

"Took it along to carry her and then turned it loose."

Dusty and Mark exchanged glances then turned their gaze back to this new Calamity. None of the trio spoke for a few moments as they turned Calamity's idea over in their heads. At last Dusty gave a shrug.

"You could be right, Calam," he said. "I've been thinking all along that Belle might have picked up word about that attack on us and rode out to warn us."

"Then why tell her folks about going to the Grayne place?" Mark inquired.

"Maybe to stop them worrying about her," Dusty suggested. "But if she didn't go out to warn us, where did she go?"

"That last time you met, Mark," Calamity said. "Did Belle tell you where she was headed?"

"No. We talked—well, we talked about a whole lot of things, but not about where she aimed to go. All I knew was that she was headed somewhere on a job."

"And she didn't say where?" Dusty asked.

"No. Just allowed that it was a big one which took some time to set up and that if it came off would be big."

"It *was* big," Dusty said. "Her paw told me she brought back twenty thousand dollars from it."

"Whooee!" Calamity breathed. "That *is* big."

"Big enough so the man who lost it wouldn't forget easy," Mark growled. "Do you think whoever she took might've——"

"It's possible," agreed Dusty.

"Lord!" Mark spat out. "I wish I'd stopped——"

"Cut that right out, Mark!" Calamity snapped. "You know Belle. Once she's made up her mind, you'd not change it. For a job that big she'd need help and she wouldn't let the said help down by not going through with it."

"That's true, Mark," Dusty said gently.

"I know it," Mark answered. "Don't her folks know anything?"

"Jack Starr said she never mentioned where she'd been——"

"Hold it!" Mark interrupted. "She started teasing me about her partner when I tried to talk her out of going——"

"And?" Dusty prompted.

"We let it drop after a spell. Then just before we parted, Belle said for me not to worry, her partner was old enough to be both our grandpappy."

"That might help Jack Starr remember something," Dusty replied. "He probably knows most of Belle's partners."

Before any more could be said, a knock sounded at the door. On being told to enter, Herb, the Kissels' hand, stepped in, jerking a thumb towards the front of the house.

"Feller coming in, Cap'n," he said.

"Anybody you know?"

"Don't ride like anybody from 'round here," the local man replied. "He's an oldish-looking cuss and dressed a mite fancy."

All three at the table came to their feet and headed for the window which looked out on to the front of the property. A man rode down the trail towards the Starr place, showing an air of alert, watchful caution Dusty for one found most interesting and significant. Although the approaching man looked to be getting on in years, he sat his horse well. He wore a low-crowned black Stetson, black frock coat of ancient line which bore signs of trail-dirt, white shirt, string tie, striped trousers, spats and town shoes. When the man drew nearer, his face showed seamed lines, yet carried an expression of sober, solemn dignity.

"Circuit riding preacher, maybe," Mark guessed.

"I'd say a law-wrangler of some kind," Calamity went on.

"Or something else!" Dusty ejaculated and turned to head for the door. "Did he see you, Herb?"

"Naw. I come in the back way."

In passing, Dusty hooked one of his Colts from the gunbelt which hung on the set of deer antlers by the door. Dashing across the hall, he jerked open the front door and went out on to the porch. On reflection later, Dusty decided that what happened next was all his own fault; a man of his considerable experience ought to have known better than spring a surprise on a feller who rode as that old cuss did.

Showing remarkable speed for so aged a looking man, the newcomer brought his horse to a halt. Still with the same speed, his hand went under his jacket and emerged holding a short-barrelled Merwin and Hulbert Army Pocket revolver. Even before Dusty could speak, the old man threw up the weapon into the aim, showing that he knew how to handle guns. Dusty dived forward from the porch, landing rolling and hearing the crack of the Merwin followed by the sound of a close-passing bullet. Even as the rider fired, he whirled his horse and set it to running away from the buildings, headed along the town trail at a gallop.

Dusty landed on his stomach, resting elbows on the ground and holding the Colt in both hands so as to take careful aim. Again Dusty saw something significant in the way the old man kept his horse swerving from side to side. Clearly the man expected lead to follow him and took precaution to ensure that he did not offer an easy target. While Dusty could shoot accurately at long range when supporting his Colt in that manner, he doubted if he could bring down the man and guarantee only to wound him so that he could be questioned about his actions.

"I'll get after him," Dusty told Mark as the blond giant and Calamity burst out of the house. "Stay on here."

"Yo!" Mark replied, giving the old cavalry answer.

Without waiting to be told, Calamity darted back to the sitting-room and returned carrying Dusty's gunbelt and carbine. Should the pursuit of the old man end in a gun fight, Dusty might need the extra range of the carbine as Calamity well knew. After strapping on his belt, Dusty took the carbine and headed for the corral on the run. Mark and Calamity followed, watching Dusty vault the rail as they headed for the gate. Even before they reached the gate, Dusty's big paint came to him and, dispensing with saddle or bridle, he went afork it with a bound. Mark had just removed the upper pole of the gate when Dusty rode towards him and the paint sailed over the second rail.

Keeping the paint at as fast a run as he could manage while riding bareback, Dusty sent it along the trail taken by the fleeing man. While the big stallion had speed to burn and stamina to keep that speed over a distance, Dusty did not force it too hard. He figured he would wear the old man's horse down, especially as it looked to have done some traveling while the paint was fresh, grain-fed and rested. After half a mile's running Dusty found himself closing the gap.

Dusty also began to feel puzzled as he studied the fleeing man. From what Mark said, Belle had been working with an oldish man on her last swindle. The oldster ahead acted in the manner of an outlaw—a badly wanted owlhoot at that. Maybe he had been Belle's partner, for his dress and appearance hinted at a less robust section of the criminal profession than robbing at a gun-point.

Which brought up two points: why had the man come to the Starr place; what made him start shooting as soon as he saw Dusty?

A further point emerged to puzzle Dusty. Why did the old man head towards Lubbock City if he should be a wanted outlaw? From the direction taken, the old man would have to cut off across the range soon if he hoped to avoid entering the town. Dusty wondered if he should try to anticipate the swing off, but decided against it. Instead, he concentrated on urging his horse on, closing the gap with his quarry at every raking stride.

After running for almost three miles, Dusty had closed the gap to about fifty yards, at which range even a Winchester carbine held true enough to halt the chase. However, Dusty found himself effectively blocked from using his carbine, even if he wished to do so. The old man made no attempt to avoid Lubbock City, in fact headed down towards the first houses of the range-country metropolis at that very moment. So Dusty did not attempt to shoot. While the Winchester Model 1873 carbine did not have the accuracy-potential of a Sharps Old Reliable buffalo gun—

which held true at ranges of over eight hundred yards—its two hundred grain .44 caliber bullet, powered by forty grains of powder, could kill at distances of a mile. Dusty knew he could not chance halting the paint, dropping from its back and shooting, for if he missed, his bullet might hit some innocent bystander in its flight through the town.

From all appearances there might be a good chance of hitting somebody, for a good-sized crowd stood on or before the Indian Nations Hotel on Main Street. Again, Dusty felt puzzled watching the old man ride into town, for his quarry made no attempt to avoid the crowd but rode straight towards it. Even as Dusty opened his mouth to yell a request for somebody in the crowd to halt the man, he saw the oldster swing by the edge of the crowd. The old man glanced towards the rear, then in turning to his front stared into the hotel. Swinging his horse around, the old man brought it to a halt before the building, tossed his reins over the hitching rail and walked with deceptive speed through the doors into the hotel.

Dusty saw this, but had a problem on his hands. While not as dangerous as the Kid's white, Dusty's paint did not take to strangers handling it. So Dusty could not allow the horse to go free while he took after the old man on foot. If a member of the crowd should try to halt the paint, that person had better be good with horses or he would wind up picking horse-shoes out of his back teeth. Dusty scanned the crowd, his lawman's instincts warning him that this was no peaceable meeting but an angry near-mob. Townsmen and local settlers formed the bulk of the crowd, but Dusty saw a welcome sight.

"Dude!" he yelled. "Hey, Dude, get a rope on my paint for me!"

A lounging, handsome young man swung from the porch. Dressed to the height of range-land fashion, the young man

still showed a speedy grasp of the situation. Having ridden
on three trail drives with Dusty as his boss, Dude learned
early that it paid to obey orders instantly when the small
Texan yelled. Swinging on to his horse, Dude shook free
his rope and headed towards Dusty. While the cowhand
wanted to ask questions, one look at Dusty's face warned
him not to waste time. Even before Dude's rope dropped
on the paint's neck, Dusty had dismounted and walked
towards the hotel porch.

All eyes turned towards the small Texan and Dusty noticed Bennet and Pilsen standing in a position of command.
While Dusty could guess at the cause of the meeting, he
did not wish to become involved. However, Pilsen appeared
to have other ideas.

"Hey, Fog!" the burly rancher growled. "We want to see
you."

"Not right now," Dusty answered, starting to go past the
man and watching the front of the hotel.

"Yeah, right now!" Pilsen spat out, catching Dusty's
carbine-loaded left arm. "We——"

While Dusty could sympathize with the settlers in their
problems, he took exception to any man laying hands on
him in such a manner. And when Dusty took exception to
something, things happened—fast.

Pivoting around, Dusty sank his right fist almost wrist-
deep into Pilsen's belly. The force of the blow drove the
air from the burly settler's lungs, sent waves of nausea
ripping into him and folded him over. Like a flash, Dusty
swung up his released left arm and drove the butt-plate of
the carbine into the side of Pilsen's neck, sending the man
staggering into the crowd. Without even a glance at Pilsen
or the settlers, Dusty carried on into the hotel.

An ominous rumble rose from the crowd; a meeting gathered to discuss the situation in the country and which had

been on the point of developing into a mob fit for any mischief. With the sheriff and his deputies searching for a little girl who had disappeared from her home, Indian-hate flared high and that fury might have been directed at Dusty, but Dude took a hand.

"Just hold it, gents!" he ordered, backing his words with the cocking of his right-hand Colt. "Cap'n Fog said 'later,' which means he's a mite busy right now and don't want stopping."

"You siding with him, cowboy?" growled Bennet.

Looking down at his gun, Dude gave a grin. "You might say that. Likewise stopping some of you gents getting hurt."

Just how the situation might have developed is hard to say. At that moment Bill Duffin and his deputies rode into view, the little girl seated on Duffin's lap. She had been blueberry picking down by the river and fell asleep in the bushes.

If Dusty heard what went on behind him, he gave no sign of it. In the hotel lobby he looked at the desk clerk.

"Where'd that feller go?"

"Upstairs after Jack Starr, Cap'n."

Bounding forward, Dusty went upstairs fast. Holding his carbine ready for use, he turned a corner into the passage at the head of the stairs. Jack Starr stood talking with the old man and both swung to face Dusty.

"Hold hard, Cap'n!" Starr yelled. "He came to warn Belle."

CHAPTER ELEVEN

Who Sent You After Belle?

"Reckon Dusty can handle it, Mark?" asked Calamity as they watched the small Texan gallop in pursuit of the old man.

"Don't you?" Mark answered.

"Figure he stands a chance of it," the girl said. "Let's go back to the house, shall we?"

"I'll see if there're any chores wanting doing."

Calamity nodded, guessing that Mark wanted to keep active so that he would not find time to start thinking of Belle and brooding again. "Why not go finish chopping the wood?"

"There aren't but a few logs left," Mark pointed out.

"Always like to see a chore well done," Calamity replied.

At that moment Herb and Mrs. Kissel came towards them. Being range-bred Mrs. Kissel knew better than make an appearance when guns roared for her presence would impede her friends' actions. The shooting had ended, Dusty Fog rode after the visitor and, woman-like, Mrs. Kissel wanted her curiosity satisfied.

"Ain't never been one to be nosey," Herb remarked before his employer's wife could speak, "so I——"

"We don't know either," Calamity interrupted.

"Huh. Man can't learn nothing around here," sniffed the cowhand. "Hey, Mark, found a couple of hosses on the range that looked a mite lame. Brought 'em in to the corral. Could use some help in looking 'em over."

"Come on then. Anything's better than chopping wood," Mark replied. "I'll go fetch my gunbelt."

"Are you expecting trouble, Mark?" Mrs. Kissel inquired.

"Just figure to be ready, should any come, Maw."

"Reckon I'll go in and load Bess's shotgun then."

While Mrs. Kissel went to take an elementary precaution, Mark headed in to collect his gunbelt. Herb turned to Calamity and asked, "Who was that feller, Calam?"

"Mark Counter!"

"Naw! The other one."

"Dusty Fog."

"Now me," growled Herb, "I'd've took 'em for Wyatt Earp and Bat Masterson."

"Oh, you mean *that* feller," grinned the girl. "Tell you, Herb, he didn't have real good manners and done went off without introducing hisself."

"Some of the company around here, I can't say I blame him."

"Left his calling card though," the girl went on, ignoring Herb's interjection and nodded to the bullet scar on the porch. Herb nodded soberly, then looked to where Mark left the house. "You're right at that," the cowhand said and wondered just how good with a gun the blond giant might be.

"Hey Calam," Mark called. "You'd best go in and get dressed."

"Land-sakes!" yelped Herb, knowing Mark did not mean for the girl to go in and don clothes, "are you expecting a war, or something?"

"Nope," Mark answered. "Only when shooting starts, it's too late to remember you aren't toting a gun."

"Was I a Christian, God-fearing gal," Calamity said soberly, "I'd shout 'Amen!' to that."

Leaving the men, Calamity entered the house and went upstairs to collect her gunbelt. She strapped on the belt, checked the loads of her rechambered Navy Colt, then slid the gun into the countered holster. Just as she left the room, Calamity saw her coiled whip on the chair. In a fight that long whip made a mighty effective weapon and no freight-driver like Calamity ever felt fully dressed without his, or her, main work-tool at hand. Picking up the whip, Calamity thrust it into her belt, then left the room.

Mark and Herb did not reach the corral. Just as they rounded the side of the house, both heard the sound of approaching horses. Not one, meaning Dusty returned; or two, announcing the small Texan brought in a prisoner; but three at least. Turning, Herb prepared to walk back and take a look at the newcomers, but Mark shot out a hand and lifted the other back.

"Let's see them afore they see us," the blond giant cautioned.

"Sure, Mark. Only put me down. I'm all growed up now. Even go out back alone unless it's a real dark night."

Looking around the corner, Mark and Herb studied the newcomers. Three men rode towards the house, one leading a pack-horse. From the way the men rode and their general attitude, Mark wondered if their presence tied in with the old man who left so hurriedly.

The man leading the pack-horse dropped its hackamore, leaving the animal behind, and all showed caution as they drew nearer to the house.

"Mean cusses," Herb breathed. "Know any of 'em?"

"I'm not sure," Mark replied. "The one who turned loose the pack-horse looks familiar. Can't just place him."

"That big, dark jasper's Keeger, Mark. He's a hired butcher. Saw him pass through town once. The other's Keeger's partner, Boone."

"And the third's Cockburn," Mark finished for Herb. "We run him out of town up to——"

Seeing the trio of approaching gunhands tense in their saddles, Mark chopped· off his words. For a moment he thought the men had caught sight of himself and Herb, but then it became apparent that they saw something which interested them before the house.

"Go through the back and come out front, Herb!" Mark ordered and the other went without wasting time.

However Herb wondered if Mark had the gun-skill necessary to handle a man of Keeger's caliber in a corpse-and-cartridge affair. Not being a gun fighting man himself, Herb caught up a shotgun Mrs. Kissel had loaded, warned the woman to stay put in the kitchen for a spell and made his way towards the front door.

Coming out of the house, Calamity saw the three men riding towards her and the slight tension her appearance brought about did not escape her. Range-wise, Calamity read the signs; a trio of hired guns; one just commonplace and nothing to worry about, but the other pair looked like pretty good quality stock.

"You live here, gal?" Keeger asked, bringing his horse to a halt. He was a tall, fairly handsome man, wore good quality range clothes and a gunbelt that hung just right for a real fast draw.

"You might say that," Calamity answered, tense and alert.

"Friend of your'n asked us to come tell you he wants to see you again," Keeger went on. "That right, Boone?"

"Right as right and that's right enough," answered the slim, sharp-featured man at Keeger's right hand, speaking in a high-pitched voice which carried a hideous rather than amusing note.

Neither of the men offered to speak to the third member

of the trio. Short, stocky, wearing cheap flashy clothes, he did not belong to their class and must have been brought along merely to handle such chores as his companions felt beneath their dignity. Of the three, Cockburn alone struck Calamity as being within her capabilities of handling.

"Who's the friend?" she asked.

"You'll know him when you get——" Keeger began.

"What if she doesn't want to go?" interrupted a voice from the corner of the building.

Keeger's party swivelled their eyes in Mark's direction as the blond giant came around the corner. Just as range-wise as Calamity, they read sign with equal facility and knew they faced a man who could likely handle his guns with some skill. Keeger studied Mark, wondering where the blond giant came into the game. While the big Texan's gunbelt hung just right, he himself dressed just a might too fancy for a working cowhand. Maybe he was some dude that Belle Starr brought in for trimming and who received the benefit of the girl's knowledge to purchase the correct Western clothing so he looked the part. From Mark, Keeger glanced at Calamity and felt puzzled. While the girl had a certain attraction, she in no way came up to the description Keeger's employer gave when sending the man to collect Belle Starr and bring her to Laramie. However, there was a more important matter than solving pretty puzzles to handle at that moment.

"If she don't want to come with us," Keeger said in a disarming tone, "that's all there's to it."

And with that he started to turn his horse to the right as if meaning to ride away. At Keeger's side, Boone also began to swing his horse away. Cockburn had never worked in the other two's company before and so did not know their play. Lacking knowledge, Cockburn stayed facing the blond giant for an instant, then saw his companions making their move and started to turn his own horse.

Twisting in the saddle, Keeger started to draw the gun which was concealed from Mark's view. Boone, knowing the play, also started to turn and bring out his Colt. The move showed smooth team work, long practice and deadly purpose. Against nine men out of ten it would have brought success—only they faced the tenth man that day.

Any doubts Herb might have felt about Mark's skill with a gun received an answer right then. Even as Keeger began his treacherous move, Mark's big right hand dipped, fingers closing around the butt of the off-side Colt. With his great size and terrific strength, Mark could handle the seven-and-a-half inch barrelled Cavalry Model Peacemaker with the ease lesser men used the five-and-a-half inch barrelled Artillery Model, or the four-and-three-quarter inch type known as Civilian Model. Out came the Colt, flowing up with that smooth effortless speed which set the expert apart from the merely good. Even as Keeger came around, gun out and ready, he looked death in the face. Mark's Colt roared and its bullet poked a .45 of an inch hole in the center of the hired killer's forehead, then shattered its way out of the rear of the skull.

Mark was in trouble. Having dealt with Keeger, he could not bring his gun around in time to handle Boone's move. Working as a team, Keeger and Boone had learned how to handle their play to perfection. Only a fraction of a second slower than his departed partner, Boone came around and his Colt slanted down in Mark's direction as death took Keeger out of the game.

The deep, coughing roar of a ten gauge shotgun almost deafened Mark and he felt the hot gush of muzzle-blast from behind him. Struck in the chest by the wicked charge of nine .32 buckshot balls, which had not yet spread far apart, Boone pitched out of his saddle and crashed to the ground an instant after Keeger landed. At the door of the house, Herb prepared to swing the shotgun around and deal with the last member of the party.

Taken by surprise, Cockburn had trouble of his own. The shooting spooked his horse and he found difficulty in staying in his saddle. Leaning forward, Calamity unhitched her whip, flipping back then sending coiling forward its twenty foot lash. Caught around the throat by the leather lash, already off balance from the startled pitching of his horse, Cockburn came down out of his saddle and crashed to the hard-packed earth before the house.

On landing, Cockburn felt his Colt slide from leather and clawed wildly at its butt. Calamity braced herself and heaved back on the whip handle. Jerking the lash savagely, Calamity pitched the man on to his face once more. Half strangled by the constriction of the whip's lash, Cockburn missed his gun butt. Through the roaring which seemed to fill his ears, he heard a voice; a cold, authoritative, masculine tone which chilled him and froze him immobile.

"Lie still, *hombre!*"

Such a voice was meant to be obeyed, so Cockburn made no further attempt to grab his gun. Instead he lifted his head from the dirt, moving slowly, and looked around him. Shock hit him as he saw his two companions sprawled out on the ground and recognized the attitudes as those of dead men. Which meant that Cockburn was left alone, alive, at the mercy of the blond giant. Already a big hand reached down and jerked up the fallen revolver, then two feet moved and collected the weapons from the bodies.

"Loose off, Calam," the blond giant ordered. "We've things to say to this jasper and he can't talk while you're choking him."

"Might talk after I've done though," replied the girl, but shook free her whip's lash and began to coil it with practiced ease.

"He'll talk, Calam gal," Mark promised and the voice brought a shiver down Cockburn's frame. "He'll surely talk, don't you fret none of that score."

In collecting the firearms, Mark had seen that the other two hired killers would be of no use for giving information. Mark had been forced to shoot to kill, and Keeger lay dead, while Herb's victim proved the old range saying, "There's always a burying with buckshot" was true. Which left Cockburn, winded and bruised a mite by his fall, chocked by the lash of Calamity's whip, but alive and in a position to tell them the answers to various important questions—always providing Cockburn would talk. Somehow Mark thought that the man might spout out answers given the right kind of inducement.

"Mark!" called Mrs. Kissel from the house. "Is everything all right?"

"Yes, ma'am," the blond giant answered.

"Who are they and what do they want?" the woman went on, opening the front door to come out.

"Just stay in there, Maw," Herb warned. "They're done, but they ain't no sight for a woman."

"Well, thank you 'most to death," Calamity put in.

"Shuckens, Calam gal," apologized Herb. "I don't count you as a wo——I mean I never——"

"You'd best quit while you're ahead," grinned the girl, then her grin faded and she turned to Mark. "What do you reckon they wanted, Mark?"

"I'm not sure, Calam," Mark replied. "But we've got somebody here who can give us the answers." He turned back to where Cockburn sat up, a scared man looking for nothing but death. "On your feet, scum!"

Cockburn obeyed, rising hurriedly and facing the two men and girl who gathered around him.

"Who sent you after Belle?" Mark asked.

"I—I don't know!" Cockburn answered.

Stepping forward, Mark swung his hand around and slapped Cockburn to the ground. The blond giant bent, caught Cockburn's right wrist in his hand and jerked the man's arm up. Raising his foot, Mark stamped the high heel of his Gaylin boot down to Cockburn's arm-pit. Then Mark began to pull on the wrist and shove down with his foot. Cockburn's face twisted in agony and his body contorted as pain hit him and the giant Texan's strength threatened to tear his arm out at the roots. Never had Cockburn felt such pain. The heel of the boot spiked under his arm, sinking into his body, as it had often dug into the earth to hold against the pull of a roped animal, and sent waves of torment through him. Yet the pain seemed to be nothing when compared with the pull of his arm as it felt that the flesh, muscles, veins and arteries were being stretched beyond endurance.

"Talk," Mark ordered, his voice brittle and deadly. "Who sent you after Belle?"

Neither Calamity nor Herb spoke or made a move to intervene as they watched Mark pull on the trapped arm and saw agony twist the sweat-soaked features of the gunman.

"I—don't know——!" Cockburn screamed.

Still Mark did not release his hold or slacken the pull. "Who sent you?" he repeated.

"He's telling you true, Mark," Calamity breathed, her face just a touch pale under its tan.

"I am!" Cockburn screeched. "As God's my witness, I'm telling the truth."

Slowly Mark opened his hands and moved the boot. Cockburn's arm fell limp and useless to the ground and he grabbed at it with his other hand, moaning in pain. Bending down, Mark laid hold of Cockburn's shirt front and hauled the man upright, setting him down hard on his feet.

"All right," Mark snapped. "Tell it!"

"K—Keeger took me on to help out on a chore. Reckon it was 'cause I know a few fellers and could get questions answered."

"What questions?"

"Where to find Deacon Connery was one. I got word that Deacon had been working with Belle there," Cockburn replied and nodded towards Calamity.

"Keeger didn't say why he wanted to find Deacon?" asked Calamity.

"Only to find you, Belle."

"You think I'm Belle Starr?" the girl gasped.

"This's the Starr place and you come—— Aren't you her?"

"Belle was killed three days back," Mark told the man.

"We didn't know that. Been four days on the trail hunting the Deacon after he run out of Guthrie. We figured he'd lead us to Belle, so we kept on his trail without him knowing."

"Why'd you want Belle?" asked Mark.

Fear leapt into Cockburn's eyes and he cowered back. "Keeger and Boone never told me. They picked me up in Cheyenne, just said they wanted to trace Belle Starr, or a gal I took to be Belle and an old cuss who I recognized from their description as the Deacon."

"What were you to do when you found Belle?" growled Mark.

"T—Take her alive and unharmed to Laramie," Cockburn croaked back. "It's—It's the living, breathing, gospel truth."

"And who's this Deacon cuss you keep talking about?" Calamity put in.

"He's an old cuss. Goes around swindling folks. Dresses and looks like an old circuit riding preacher, or sometimes reckons to be a lawyer who's got a will that'll give somebody a fair piece of money. Sells it to the highest bidder. He's a right smart old cuss is the Deacon."

Mark, Calamity and Herb exchanged glances at the man's words. All remembered the old man whose hectic visit preceded the arrival of Keeger's trio and who had fled across the ranges with Dusty in hot pursuit. With Keeger and Boone dead and Cockburn so terrified that he did not dare lie, that old man might be the only lead to whoever sent the killers after Belle.

"He must have been Belle's partner!" Calamity gasped.

"Yeah," Mark agreed. "Knowing this bunch were after him explains why he acted as he did when Dusty came out of the——"

"Dusty went after him!" Calamity interrupted.

"Yeah, and's likely to catch up with him," Mark replied. "That old feller's the answer to all our questions, Calam."

Only both knew that the old man might take his knowledge to a grave should he try to make a fight when Dusty caught up with him.

CHAPTER TWELVE

I Want to Find a Man

Since leaving the Starr place that morning, the Ysabel Kid had covered some sixty miles through the reservation lands of the Indian Nations. Holding his horses at a fast walk, changing mounts regularly so as to keep something in reserve should speed of flight or pursuit become necessary, he traveled as a raiding Indian brave; as the supreme Indian raider of them all, a Comanche Dog Soldier. Yet he did not ride blindly, but instead used all the caution of the most deadly of the fighting Comanche lodges, training handed to him by men who fought the white-eye long-knife soldiers and brought practical wisdom to their teachings.

Twice during the day, sight and sound sent him into cover from which he watched unseen as small groups of Indians rode by. In each case the party consisted of young bucks from various tribes with a fair proportion of town-dressed men of the type one associated with mission schools—or that fancy college down Lubbock way. Both parties headed in a northwesterly direction, but the Kid took time out to follow neither. While interested in where the Indians might be going, he had a more important task on hand, the finding of Blue Duck and maybe the killer of Belle Starr. To do this, the Kid must not be swayed from his purpose or taken from his proposed course of action.

If he hoped to gain the necessary information and assistance, the Kid knew he must go prepared in the correct manner for the meeting and that would not be easy the way things stood in the Indian Nations.

In the East a group of people, the kind who invest any minority group with multiple good qualities of human behavior, tried to sponsor the legend that the Indian was a natural born conservationist where wild life was concerned, and blamed the white man alone for the disappearance of the game herd of the West. The Kid knew this theory to be wrong. Sure the white man killed off game, but so did the Indian. Often a tribe of Indians would run a big herd of buffalo over a cliff, find that recovering the meat would be a problem, so go after another herd. A lone buck would kill a seven hundred to thousand pound elk, take a few cuts of meat and ride on leaving the rest of the animal as fodder for the turkey-buzzards. Give an Indian a repeating rifle, put him near a herd of deer or antelope and he would shoot the gun empty, dropping does, fawns, spike-antlered and grown bucks with equal indiscrimination. No sir, the Indian had never been a conservationist where game was concerned.

That fact showed during the Kid's ride across an area which had once been rich in all kinds of natural fauna. He saw only the lesser animal forms, rabbits, prairie-dogs and such creatures too small to attract any but the most hungry Indian's attention and none of which would serve his purpose for the business ahead.

Evening drew on, the sun sinking in the west and still the Kid rode in a caution line across the range. Something moved down to the south and instantly the Kid turned his head to take a closer look at the thing which caught the corner of his eye. What he saw brought a sigh of satisfaction from him and he bent down to slide his rifle from its saddle-boot.

A small bunch of Kansas whitetail deer came stepping daintily and cautiously from a small wooded area. While the animals were not as large as the Texas variety to which the Kid had long been accustomed, they still made a mighty pretty picture and offered him a solution to his problem. Seeing the deer seemed like a sign that *Ka-Dih* watched over the Kid and approved of his plan. However, there remained one slight detail. He must get close enough to those wary, much-hunted animals so that he could down the big buck. And it must be the buck; not because of its rat-rack spread of antlers, but because buck's meat would be needed for his plan's success.

Slipping from his saddle, the Kid surveyed the situation. One thing he knew for certain, he could not ride any closer to that wary bunch of deer. Which meant he must move in on foot—or on his belly, for there was no chance of getting too close while erect, not in that kind of cover.

Leaving his horse standing in a hollow, the Kid advanced in a stooping crouch. He gripped the rifle in both hands, held down before him but ready for instant use. Knowing the limitations of the Winchester, the Kid wanted to get in to at least a hundred yards before he chanced shooting. While the Winchester carried a leaf rear sight adjustable to ranges of one thousand yards and would kill at that distance, the Kid knew that only pure, blind luck would enable an aimed shot to strike its mark beyond four hundred yards. With its comparatively light forty grain powder load—no greater than that in the old Dragoon at the Kid's side—the Winchester rifle did not offer great long range accuracy; nor had it been built for such work, but as a light, handy long arm with good magazine capacity, and as such the Model '73 could not be equalled.

Darting from cover to cover, the wind blowing from the deer towards him, the Kid managed to get within a hundred and fifty yards of the deer. Then he saw the big buck come around, head raised and pointing his way. Instantly the Kid froze like a statue. For a full minute he remained without a single movement, waiting until the buck resumed feeding. However, the Kid knew the danger. Once alerted, the buck would not soon relax its vigilance. There would be no chance of getting in any closer to the herd.

Slowly the Kid sank to the ground, going down on his stomach and lying spread out so as to keep as far out of sight as possible. Moving with the same slow and deliberate care, he moved his hat and slid it before him, then inched the rifle forward and rested it upon the Stetson's crown. Cuddling the butt-plate to his shoulder, the Kid took careful aim, flipping up and adjusting the sight for the range, then laying the rested rifle on the big buck.

A doe moved between the buck and the Kid's rifle and a low hiss of annoyance left his lips. At any moment the buck might spook, or the herd feed back into the woods where he would never manage to get close enough for a shot. Knowing the Indian Nations, the Kid doubted if he could find any other living game within miles and did not wish to take the time to search for it.

At last the doe moved and once more the tip of the foresight settled in line with the buck's shoulder. Gauging the wind and sighting with all his care, the Kid gently squeezed the trigger. He barely heard the sharp crack of exploding powder or felt the recoil push against his shoulder. Burnt powder smoke obscured his view for a moment, but his every instinct told him he held true. And he did. The buck jumped high as lead smashed into it, landing running, took four strides then staggered and went sprawling down. On the shot's sound reaching them, every doe went leaping swiftly into the woods, their tails flashing like white fans as they fled.

The Kid felt a touch of pity as he whistled up his horses and rode to where the buck lay dead. Likely that was the last male in the area, at least the last grown male, the does would scatter, looking for mates instead of the other way around. That might be a good thing, taking them to an area where they could stand a chance of growing and breeding families.

"Sorry old-timer," he said as he loaded the buck's body on to one of his relay. "Least it came quick and painless and you'll be real useful."

With the deer loaded, the Kid swung afork his white stallion and rode away from the area. Night came, but the Kid carried on in an unerring manner. At around ten o'clock that night he came in sight of a clump of buildings, the place he sought. Down below where he sat lay the village housing most of the big-name chiefs of the fighting Indian tribes. There the Kid would find what he required.

From where he sat, the Kid spent a moment studying the scene below him; the small cabins, well-built and comfortable enough, but firm anchored to the ground in a way no tepee ever had been. A man could not change his campsite with a wooden cabin and the Kid could guess how those free-ranging war leaders must feel to be held in one place. In the center of the village a fire glowed and men sat around it; the man the Kid came to see among them most likely. With that in mind, the Kid prepared to ride down in the time-honored and traditional manner. Only by doing so could he hope to achieve his purpose.

Taking his rifle from the saddleboot, the Kid fired a shot into the air. Flicking down the lever, he left the action open and removed his right hand. Holding the gun by its foregrip in his left hand, he raised it over his head. Then he slowly rode down the slope towards the village.

They sat around the fire, old men in cast-off white-eye clothing. Yet once they had led warrior bands and spread terror across the Western plains. White Wind of the Kaddo;

Lone Bar, war chief of the Southern Cheyenne; Plenty Kills who took the fighting Kiowa through a regiment of U.S. cavalry and routed it; old Bone Breaker from the Waco tribe; once their names made even the most hardy and battle-wise Texans wish for stout protective walls and a plentiful supply of powder and shot. The others at the fire, from Northern and Western tribes, also bore names well known and all could claim to be a respected leader of his people.

And now they sat around a fire in Oklahoma Territory, living on hand-outs from the Government at the beck and call of every two-bit agent in the Nations. At such a moment the Kid hated having white blood and everything the white race stood for in its handling of Indians. Yet he forced himself to go on with the ritual.

"I come in peace, with an empty gun and bringing meat for your woman's cooking pots," he said in fluent Comanche, halting his horse in the light of the fire.

None of the old men about the fire moved. Cold, impersonal eyes studied the Kid and thought him to be a joke-playing cowhand who had in some way learned the old conventional ritual and sought to mock them by using it.

"Many winter ago, Plenty Kills," the Kid went on in English, "a war chief cuts wrists with you, each swearing to the Great Spirit that he and all his family would always have the right to ask and receive from the other."

A seamed old face looked up, eyes bright and keen as on that day, more than thirty years gone by, when he took the blood oath. First he studied the Kid's obviously white man's clothing and equipment, then looked at the horses, took in the buck's body and finally lifted to the Indian-dark, young looking face, examining its features carefully.

"Who speaks of this?" asked Plenty Kills.

"My people call me *Cuchilo*, the Knife," replied the Kid. "My mother was one called Raven Head. Her father bore an honored name which I have never disgraced—I speak the name—Long Walker of the Dog Soldier Lodge," he paused for a couple of seconds then went on, "My people are the *Tshaoh*."

"The *Tshaoh!*" breathed White Wind.

"The Enemy People!" muttered Lone Bear and then sat nodding his head in approval as if he had never doubted which tribe sired this dark young man.

"The Comanche!" rumbled several other voices.

All three names ran around the circle of the fire, yet they meant but one thing, the title of the greatest horse-Indians of them all. Every eye stayed on the tall young man. No longer did the crowd regard him as an interloper, but in the light of his being an honored visitor from another tribe who came on important and urgent business, yet retained sufficient good manners to come correctly and in the traditional way.

"Come to my lodge, grandson of my blood-brother," invited Plenty Kills.

Dropping from his saddle, the Kid followed the old man away from the fire. Mutters of admiration rose as the chief studied the great white stallion which followed the Kid like a huge hound-dog, leading the relay horses behind it. Old tongues ran across lips as the chiefs studied the big buck hanging from one saddle. It had been long since meat came their way and all knew Plenty Kills would share his bounty with them.

The inside of Plenty Kills' cabin looked like the interior of a tepee. In the center of the room a fire blazed, sending its smoke through the hole in the roof. Skin beds lay around the walls, a Winchester rifle in its medicine cover leaned against one corner and a bow, quiver of arrows and war lances faced it from across the room. Kneeling by the fire, a plump, white-haired old squaw turned her gaze to the door as Plenty Kills entered followed by the Kid.

"This is grandson of my old brother, Long Walker," announced the chief. "He brings meat for you to cook. Make food for him."

"Long Walker great warrior, plenty man," replied the old woman, looking at the Kid with life sparkling in her eyes. "Gave me fine son. Take many coups, bring much prizes from war. Have two long-knife soldiers before him when Great Spirit take him at the battle on the Prairiedog Fork of the Brazos."

The words did not surprise or shock the Kid. Back in the old days a guest who traveled alone would be given *all* the comforts of home and the depth of his welcome could be gauged by which of the host's squaws found herself assigned to satisfy his needs. Should a child result from the satisfying, it received no different treatment than regular members of the family and bore no stigma of shame.

"Make food, Drinking Antelope," grunted Plenty Kills. "I regret I have no squaw to make your bed this night, *Cuchilo.*"

"You come a full thirty winters too late," chuckled the squaw and left the cabin. Outside came a scuffling sound, followed by the yelp of a stricken dog.

"What help do you need, *Cuchilo?*" asked Plenty Kills, ignoring the sound.

"I want to find a man."

"His name?"

"Blue Duck," the Kid answered and his mouth watered a little as he thought of what the dog's yelp meant. Quickly he told Plenty Kills of the trouble around Lubbock and his reason for wanting to find the man named.

Plenty Kills did not answer for some time. Squatting on his heels, he looked long and hard into the flames. At last he turned to the Kid and troubled lines showed on his face.

"There is a bad spirit in this land, *Cuchilo*. Plenty trouble comes soon. Aiee! No man lives for ever and why should an old man chief of a great tribe take orders from one who has never been a brave-heart?" Clearly the last words were direct to himself, not the Kid, for Plenty Kills went on, "I will ask questions."

Neither the Kid nor Plenty Kills noticed that the squaw had entered as they spoke. Her eyes flickered to them as she took up a cooking pot and she walked out of the cabin without speaking. Coming to his feet, Plenty Kills left the room and the Kid remained in a heel-squat by the fire. Time dragged by, Drinking Antelope entered once more and set her pot on the flames, kneeling by it while she stirred the contents.

"What bad spirit fills your people?" asked the Kid.

"A young one comes, with many fine words," she replied. "He talked with the old man chiefs, and swore them to an oath of silence. I know no more, save that many young fools gather to that one's war lance. There will be many of our people die in following a false dream. Do you have a squaw, *Cuchilo?*"

"No."

"Every young brave-heart needs a squaw to care for him."

And with that the old woman turned her attention to the cooking pot, crooning tonelessly. The Kid knew he would learn nothing more from her and sat in silence to await Plenty Kills' return.

"I pass word," the chief remarked. "May take small time to get word, but we find Blue Duck for you."

"The man I want may be mixed in with your oath of silence. I won't hold you to your blood oath if that is so."

Gratitude glowed in the old man's eyes, then Plenty Kills' face split in a warm smile. "You fit grandson of Long Walker. But the blood oath is higher than one taken at knife point. I get word to you. Where I send word?"

No white man, even one with Indian blood in his veins, could set up residence on the reservation lands without permission from the Indian Affairs Bureau and the Kid had no wish to notify them of his presence.

"Not a mile from here is a small wood, with water for your horses. Make camp there and I send Drinking Antelope with food."

"So be it," grunted the Kid, falling easily into the Comanche tongue.

"You eat first," the squaw ordered, "or have you taken the white-eye's way of not touching the flesh of dog?"

A grin creased the Kid's face. While he still retained his taste for dog-stew cooked Indian style, he rarely found chance to indulge in the delicacy when on the OD Connected. So he told the woman he still enjoyed the food and settled down to a good meal. After eating well, he left the cabin, collected his horses and rode off in the direction indicated by the old chief.

On his arrival at the wood, the Kid found a small clearing and made his preparations for a stay that might last for a couple of days. To make sure that anybody who came to see him could arrive unharmed, the Kid took his horses down stream and left them hobbled on good grazing, even the big white stallion. Then he returned to the clearing and made a fire-less camp. Just as he was spreading his blankets, he heard a twig snap. Instantly his hand went to the hilt of his bowie knife.

"Cuchilo!" said a low, feminine voice.

"Who speaks?" he answered.

"Drinking Antelope sent me. She said you want Blue Duck."

"Come ahead—slow and easy!"

Crouching down, knife in hand, the Kid watched the

approaching shape. Taken with the voice, that slim figure would belong to a girl in her late teens. She moved light on her feet and showed no fear. Not even when the Kid loomed up at her side, catching her arm in his and holding it while keeping the knife point against her ribs.

"Who are you?" he repeated.

"They call me Rainey Smith," the girl replied. "You have no need to fear me. I came to help you find Blue Duck."

"Why?"

The Kid figured that if Rainey Smith had been in with the three shapes which burst into view from the bushes, she would have talked louder, making her voice cover the slight noise they created in their advance. Give them their due, that trio moved pretty well and the first of them had come mighty close before the Kid became aware of his presence.

Thrusting the girl away from him, the Kid prepared to deal with the menace to his life and well-being. The nearest attacker held a rifle, the Kid could not yet see how the other two—or was it three?—were armed. Flinging himself forward in a rolling dive, the Kid went under the gun's bullet. Ignoring the sting of muzzle flame, he came up alongside the rifle, heard its user working the lever, and his knife sank home. Deep into the attacker's stomach drove the razor-sharp blade and ripped across. As he struck, the Kid twisted his head to see the second attacker looming up and starting to throw a rifle to his shoulder. No fool this one, he meant to take aim and not miss his shot.

A flood of intestines gushed from the first man's laid-open belly, trailing over the Kid's hand and wrist, tangling it and holding it for a vital instant. It looked like *Ka-Dih* had given up on the Kid, for he could not clear his hand in time. Then he saw a dark shape leap forward, an arm lashing at the rifle and another locking around its user's throat. The rifle went off, but its bullet flew into the air harmlessly.

Rainey Smith hung on the attacker's back, pulling down on the rifle and clinging despite the man's attempt at shaking her free.

With a jerk, the Kid tore his hand free, the weight of the body falling over backwards helped drag the trailing mass of intestines away. He sprang to meet the next attacker just as the man threw Rainey to one side. Although the man sent the girl staggering, he acted an instant too late. Before he could get his rifle up, he went to the Land of Good Hunting; sent on his way by a roundhouse slash of the James Black bowie laying bare his throat almost to the bone.

The Kid whirled to meet his last attacker—if he had counted right at only three. Across the clearing the third man suddenly arched his back, stumbled and went down, his rifle dropping from his hands.

"You fight as good as Long Walker, *Cuchilo*," came Plenty Kills' voice from the blackness.

"Did you send the gal?" asked the Kid, pleased with the compliment but getting down to business.

"My squaw sent her. Make plenty bad mistake. They have been watching Rainey Smith for days now. You best get horse and go, *Cuchilo*. This will not be good place to be soon. And you must take Rainey Smith with you. If you don't, she dead before next sun go down."

CHAPTER THIRTEEN

We've Found 'em,
Now We've Got a Problem

"You'd best tell me why she came first," the Kid said.

"I speak English," the girl answered. "I hate all these young ones. They killed my father when he stood against their plans."

"Rainey speaks true words, *Cuchilo*," the chief confirmed, plucking his war axe from the body of the Kid's third attacker. "Black Eagle found dead. Reservation police, those three there, say accident while cleaning his rifle— only hole in his back. Trust the girl, *Cuchilo*, take her at least to a safe place with you."

"How about you?" asked the Kid.

"They not know I've been here. And I am still Plenty Kills. Man know, as I am not easily killed. Make much stink, young ones not want stink, bring in my good friends Madsen, Tilghman and Thomas."

The Kid grinned, seeing that the chief would be safe. The three named were U.S. marshals and famed for their ability at keeping the law and solving crimes. If the "Three Guardsmen," as they were known, were friends of Plenty Kills, he would be safe—and the Kid figured the old chief could still handle his end in a fight, especially against reservation-softened young bucks.

"What'll you say about these three?" the Kid inquired.

"Not be here to say anything. If men ask in morning, well, I been among white men long enough to know how to lie. Say I know nothing, except maybe they get dead by accident while sharpening knives and war axe. Ride careful, *Cuchilo*—but ride fast, far and now."

In the distance shouts sounded and the Kid knew that people would soon be coming, men wanting to investigate the shooting and with the desire to avenge dead comrades when they learned the cause.

"Let's go, gal," he said.

"The name's Rainey," she replied.

"I'll mind it. Now get going. My thanks for your help, Plenty Kills."

"It was the oath. Speak well of me to Long Walker when next you meet. Tell him he has a worthy grandson."

Turning without another word, the old man faded off into the darkness and the Kid felt pleased that Plenty Kills had not been stalking him. Only there was no time to stand around thinking. Happen the Kid figured to grow up and be all old and ornery, he must put some miles between him and the woods before daylight.

With the girl gliding at his side, the Kid made his way to where he left his horses. Even without telling, she started to saddle one animal while the Kid tossed his rig on to the white stallion. Working fast, he and the girl soon had all three horses prepared for riding. Long before the first of the searchers reached the woods, the Kid and the girl were riding north-west at a good speed.

Not until five miles of winding, hard to track distance lay between them and the woods did the Kid slow down his horse. For a time Rainey and he rode in silence, then the girl asked, "Do you trust me?"

"Reckon I do, or you'd be dead back there. Only I want to know more about why you're helping me."

"Let's make camp soon, we can't reach the young ones' camp tonight."

"Sure, gal."

Half an hour later, by a small fire's light, the Kid took his first good look at Rainey Smith. A feeling of shock hit him as he came from tending the horses and saw her in the fire's light. Although the hair was Indian black instead of red, and she wore a plain doe-skin dress instead of shirt and jeans, that might have been Comanche Blade standing before him. Maybe not identical in features, but with the same wild beauty about her as the one girl in the Kid's life always showed. There was the same calm competence in the way the girl made coffee over an open fire and grilled some meat the Kid brought from the Starr place.

"Hope you don't mind me looking," the girl said. "Only we'd best eat now, it'll not be safe to show smoke in daylight, they'll be after us for sure."

"Want you bad, huh?" asked the Kid.

"I know the whole game. They'd've killed me weeks back only they knew the old man chief wouldn't stand for it and I never went any place they could arrange an accident. Are you working for the Government?"

"Should I be?" asked the Kid.

"We have to trust each other, *Cuchilo,*" she pointed out.

"Then you tell your side of it first."

Without halting her work, Rainey started to talk about herself. Born of a red father and captive white mother, she grew up in a Kaddo camp. Her mother died while the girl still crawled and her father went under in battle against the cavalry. So, as was the Indian custom, Rainey found herself adopted by Black Eagle, one of the lesser old man chiefs. She had been treated as one of the family and when the tribe moved to the Indian Nations reservation, she came along. Life had not been easy, but still fairly happy until a month or so back.

While interested in the girl's story to that point, the Kid realized the part which concerned him must be coming up.

So it proved. Rainey told how one of the college Indians visited their village and spoke long with the old man chiefs, claiming that a new war leader had risen, one with such good medicine that he would lead all the Indian Nations to victory over the white man. Would then the leaders of the tribes give their support? Such a decision could not be reached without much talk around the council fire and her father—she regarded Black Eagle in that light—spoke loudest against the futility of the plan and pointed out that others made the same claim, only to see their medicine broken and many lives lost. That night the old chief left his cabin to stroll on the edge of the village. When he did not return, a search party went out and found his body, shot in the back. The reservation police said he died in an accident while cleaning his gun.

Black Eagle died without a son to avenge him, but Rainey set out to do so. Just how she managed it, the girl did not say, but she learned plenty about this new leader and his war medicine. Mission-educated, she used a brain trained to think backed by a woman's wiles and wormed secrets from the men behind the medicine plan in her village. Only in doing so she must have aroused suspicions, for a change came over the men. No longer did they speak freely before her, but watched her all the time. From that moment she lived balanced on a razor's edge. Only the fact that Plenty Kills appointed himself unofficial guardian saved her, but she knew that the moment she left the village, she would die.

Then the Kid came to the village and Drinking Antelope told the girl of his mission. Believing herself unwatched, Rainey slipped out of the camp, hoping to trade her knowledge for his protection until she could reach the authorities and warn them of their danger.

"Will you take me?" she asked.

"After I've seen Blue Duck," answered the Kid.

"He may be dead," she warned. "Only this afternoon one of the men you killed came back from their secret camp and I heard him telling the others that their big leader sent word to hold Blue Duck until he visited them."

"I aim to find him," the Kid stated. "How do I find this camp?"

"It is in Antelope Canyon, in the foothills. I take you. Now eat your food so I can put out the fire."

They ate in silence and at last, the meal over, the Kid asked, "What'll you do after this's over?"

"I don't know," Rainey answered. "There is nothing to go back to." She studied him for a moment, then went on, "Are you married?"

"Nope. Go get the blankets and bed down over there."

"You only have three blankets, what will you do?"

"I'll get by," grunted the Kid.

Rising, Rainey went to where the blankets hung strapped to one of the saddles. She returned, halting at the Kid's side and spreading the blankets on the ground by the embers of the fire.

"You will be stiff with cold in the morning, *Cuchilo*," she said quietly. "And that would not be good. If we divide the blankets, both will be cold."

"It only leaves us one choice then," the Kid replied. "Doesn't it?"

The first tinge of dawn crept into the sky and the Kid stirred, feeling the warmth of the girl against him. Raising himself on one elbow, he looked down at her and she opened her eyes. Slowly her arms crept around his neck and drew his face down to her own.

"This is one thing the white folks do that beats any Indian way," she told him and their lips met in a long, passionate kiss. "Perhaps we don't see another night, *Cuchilo*."

"Maybe not. Is there anything you'd like to do in case we don't?"

"Only one thing," she breathed and the Kid found he could easily grant her wish.

For most of the day Rainey led the Kid across a section of the Indian Nations he had never seen before. While riding, the Kid kept a careful watch on their backtrail and picked a route which would make following their tracks a slow and difficult process. He found the girl a handy companion for such a mission. Rainey had tended to be something of a tomboy and rode with the village youths as a child, absorbing their lessons. Once as he watched their backtrail, the girl spotted a small band of Indians in the distance, enabling her and the Kid to take cover and avoid being seen. Twice more during the day they hid from sight of small Indian bands and the Kid noticed a significant fact. The Indians all appeared to be going in the same direction that he and the girl traveled.

Just before sundown Rainey suggested they leave the horses hidden in a draw as the canyon they sought lay beyond the next rim of the foothills through which they had been traveling for the last two hours. Accepting the girl's judgment, the Kid obeyed. Knowing he could rely on his relay to keep quiet, he left the horses standing and grazing while he and the girl picked their way cautiously up the slope.

"Know how to use a gun, Rainey?" he asked before they moved.

"A rifle," she agreed.

The Kid then did something neither of his friends would have believed had they seen it. Drawing his much-prized Winchester from the saddleboot, he handed it to the girl.

"Don't blow my leg off with it," he told her and she poked her tongue out at him, then started up the slope.

On reaching the top of the rise, they flattened down in cover and peered at what lay below. The Kid figured that the half-circle of five cabins had been built by white men, outlaws most likely, although the buildings looked in a poor state of repair. Beyond the buildings lay a broken-fenced corral which had no horses. Several tepees scattered before the houses and in the center of the area squaws built a pile of timber for a medicine fire. The company around the camp interested both the Kid and Rainey, mission or college students mingled with a bunch of as mean bad-hat bucks as could be found. Pawnee, Osage and Crow rubbed shoulders with Cheyenne, Kaddo, Sioux——

"And dog-my-cats if there's not some Apaches down there. New Mexico and Arizona Apaches at that," growled the Kid.

"This must be the gathering when the tribes who don't live on the Indian Nation lands are to meet the big chief, the one with the medicine," Rainey replied. "I did not known it was to come. What now, Lon?"

"There you've hit it, gal," he grinned back. "We've found 'em, now we've got a problem. How—— Hey, look there!"

Following the Kid's pointing finger, Rainey saw an Indian girl carrying a bowl of food into a cabin, but more significantly, a couple of rifle armed braves went in with her, each acting like he expected trouble."

"Perhaps it's Blue Duck," Rainey said.

"It's a prisoner of some kind, that's for sure," answered the Kid and his eyes went to where, on the other slope, a bunch of horses grazed. "Now I'd say I've got me a fool idea, Rainey gal."

Moving through the darkness down the slope, the Kid started to put his plan into operation. From what he had seen of Rainey Smith all that day, the girl could handle her end of the affair. All he needed to do was take care of his part. In his right hand he held his old Dragoon, in the left, blade at his side, he carried the bowie knife.

Clearly the Indians thought their camp must be safe for they had no guards out and all attention centered on the man who stood by the medicine fire. Despite the long, flowing eagle-feather war bonnet, fancy buckskins and medicine-cased rifle, the Kid recognized Joseph Three-Feathers. From the way that bunch of bucks sat in silence, the college Indian spoke some mighty interesting words. Drawing closer, the Kid could hear Three-Feathers speaking and learned much Rainey could not tell him about the new medicine of the coming war leader.

"Soon my medicine will be proved!" Three-Feathers shouted. "Soon the white man will be driven from this land, leaving it to the Indians. Then, free from white spies, we can prepare for the big war which will drive the white dogs into the sea."

"Where are your coups, your loot to show of success?" asked a thick-bodied Apache and his party gave low grunts of agreement.

"Yes," boomed a tall Sioux wearing cast-off cowhand clothing. "All we have done so far is drive off cattle and horses, roll a rock at a stagecoach and set fire to a barn. Where is the honor in that?"

"Soon the honor will come," Three-Feathers answered. "But we must make the white man attack us first. That is why we strike only when the rain will hide our tracks. Only once did somebody go against my word by attacking white men, and the Great Spirit gave them bad medicine so that many died."

"Neat the way he's using Dusty, Mark and me to build him up," mused the Kid, and reached the corner of the first hut.

"Then why do we do such things?" asked the Sioux.

"I know white people," Three-Feathers explained. "In Washington there are white fools who will believe any story an Indian tells. When the settlers attack us, they will hear only that there was nothing to prove Indians caused the bad things to happen and will lay all the blame on the white settler. Even if we kill every white man in the Nations, those fools will stand strong for us. This I know to be true. So we make bad things happen until the settlers attack, then we strike back."

Give him his due, thought the Kid, Three-Feathers could sure hold a crowd's attention and painted a mighty rosy picture of the future. In the past, the Indian tribes fought singly against the white soldiers and fell in turn. At that point, Three-Feathers used the Custer defeat on the Little Big Horn to illustrate how a merging of only two tribes brought victory. If every tribe united, they could drive the white men from their lands.

Giggles from the cabin he was passing brought the Kid to a halt. He peeped in through the window and saw a group of young Indians standing by the door and watching the meeting. The next cabin proved to be unoccupied and just as the Kid started to dart across the open space between the building and the one which he suspected held Blue Duck, he heard a sound which brought him to a sudden halt.

The call of a common nighthawk came as a bird flitted through the sky in search of food. For a moment the Kid froze, cursing the luck, but the bird did not call again. While making their plans, Rainey and the Kid had settled on the nighthawk's call repeated three times as the signal which brought her side of the business into operation.

On reaching the next cabin, the Kid halted outside. He stood listening, straining his keen ears to try to catch any sound of danger. Only one low hiss of breathing reached the Kid's ears and he carefully raised his head. A small fire burned in the center of the room, and laid out on the floor, roped up securely as only an Indian could do it, was a tall young man whose cowhand style clothing showed signs of rough handling and who was pure redman despite his dress.

Luckily the rear window had neither glass nor frame left, for the Kid had no wish to make a noise in his entrance to the cabin. Swinging his leg over the window ledge, the Kid slipped into the room. He saw the Indian's head swing in his direction and moved fast. Two strides carried him to the prisoner's side and the blade of the bowie knife moved into place for the instant slitting of the throat.

"I've come to get you out of here," the Kid said. "You want to come?" The Indian nodded vigorously. "All right, I'll cut you free, but happen you aim to make a sound, sing your death song real quick."

"Who sent you?" asked the Indian in a whisper, as the Kid's knife slashed his bonds.

"Mister, I'd say you wasn't in any position to be worrying over that," answered the Kid dryly. "Are you Blue Duck?"

"Yes—— Hey, did Belle Starr send you?"

Studying Blue Duck's face, the Kid decided that nobody could be so good an actor as to make that remark and have it sound just right if the speaker possessed knowledge of Belle's death. For a moment Blue Duck's features remained showing a look of interest, then grimaced as pain caused by restored circulation of the blood bit into him. The Indian tried to rise, but could not. However, no sound left his lips and the Kid laid a gentle knife-filled hand on the other's shoulder.

"Just rest there for a spell. I'll tend to anybody who comes through the door."

Ten minutes ticked by. Outside the cabin, Three-Feathers boomed on, painting a glowing picture of the brave new world awaiting all who followed his brave plan, hinting at the fate of such as did not side him and occasionally answering a question thrown by one of the audience. At last Blue Duck dragged himself to his feet and limped across to the window.

"I can walk now," he said.

Leaning out of the window, the Kid gave a near-perfect impersonation of the call of a common nighthawk. Three times he gave the call, then he waited to see how well Rainey Smith carried out her part of the plan.

On the rim behind the horse herd, Rainey heard the signal. Kicking her heels into the ribs of her mount, she sent it bounding forward and down the slope. She let out a wild yell and, steering the horse with her knees, its reins looped around the saddlehorn, she levered three shots into the air. Already made restless by the fire and the fuss below, the horses in the herd needed little encouragement to set them running. The horse herd guards had been slack, watching the meeting rather than tending to their duties. Although all stayed on their mounts, they could not halt the wild stampede. Rainey only started the horses running, then swung her mount away and the guards did not follow her, being more interested in trying to retrieve the stampede. If any man had followed the girl, he most likely would have died, for she knew how to handle a rifle.

At the fire every man came bounding to his feet on hearing Rainey's attack on the horses. Like cowhand, an Indian preferred any traveling he did to be from the back of a horse; and the council was forgotten as the men heard their mounts scatter. Letting out wild yells, every Indian with the exception of Three-Feathers went bounding up the slope, shouting for the guards to catch the fleeing horses.

Watching the departure of his audience, Three-Feathers let out a snarl of fury. He heard the excited chatter of the girls and turned to find them streaming out of the cabin. Just as he bellowed an order for the girls to get back inside, he saw movement in the darkness beyond the buildings. A pair of horses, riderless but wearing white-men's saddles, came out of the darkness—one of them a huge white stallion. Three-Feathers recognized the horse and fury gripped him. In some manner one of the Texans who had done so much to spoil his plans—Dusty Fog's name had been much used by Sheriff Duffin in stopping settler-made trouble—must have found the meeting. Then Three-Feathers realized where the horses headed for, and he saw two human forms, one moving slowly and painfully, emerge from the rear of a cabin towards the horses. It was the cabin where the prisoner had been held and Blue Duck knew too much to be allowed to escape.

Jerking the medicine cover off the weapon across his arm, Three-Feathers let out a wild war yell and bounded forward. In that moment the thin veneer of white man's education and civilization left Three-Feathers and he became a pure and simple savage—only he no longer possessed an Indian's speed of reactions.

"Behind you!" Blue Duck yelled as he dragged himself on to the second horse.

The Kid whirled around, his right hand twisting palm out to fetch the old Dragoon from leather. Flame belched from Three-Feathers' gun but he fired on the run which was not conducive to accuracy. Raising his Dragoon shoulder high and in both hands, the Kid took aim and fired. The roar of his old Colt echoed Three-Feathers' shot and drowned out Blue Duck's yelp of pain. Even though startled at what he saw when Three-Feathers fired at him, the Kid aimed true. Caught in the chest by the soft round lead ball, Three-Feathers not only halted in his stride, he pitched over backwards as if struck by a charging buffalo.

"Let's go!" yelled the Kid, whirling and making a flying mount on to his white. "You hurt bad?"

"I—It's nothing," Blue Duck replied, dragging himself on to his horse and clutching at where blood oozed through his pants' leg. "I can ride."

"Then do it!" the Kid ordered, his voice grim as he thought of Three-Feathers' weapon and how Belle Starr had been killed.

Yells and bellows mingled with the screaming of the girls and some of the local men started to come back instead of haring up the slope and screaming abuse at the herd guards. They left their return too late. All heard the drumming of departing hooves but by the time they reached the cabin, whoever came, released the prisoner and killed their leader, had long gone.

There could be no pursuit unless the herd guards managed to recapture some of the scattered horses. Even with an immediate return there would be little chance of following before dawn brought light enough to read tracks.

And then came the final proof that Three-Feathers no longer had the Great Spirit's approval. Rain started to fall, a few spots at first, but building up into a steady downpour. With that thought in mind, the assembled Indians decided to forget the entire affair and, when the herd guards managed to gather their horses, split up to go their separate ways.

Far to the south-east, the Ysabel Kid, Rainey Smith and Blue Duck found a cave in which to shelter from the rain. In the light of a fire Rainey examined the Indian's wound.

"It's only small," she said.

"Real small," agreed the Kid and looked at Blue Duck. "You was lucky, friend, real lucky. That gun Three-Feathers used fired buckshot."

CHAPTER FOURTEEN

Cap'n Fog's Strategy

On the evening of the Kid's departure from the Starr place, a meeting was held in the sitting-room of the house. Dusty Fog brought Deacon Connery and the cowhand Dude out from town with him, and along with Mark and Calamity they gathered around the table to discuss Belle's killing.

"I reckon we can forget the feller who hired Keeger's bunch, Mark," Dusty stated. "Deacon here can tell you about it."

Clearing his throat, and looking as sober as if about to plead with a jury to find for his client, the old man began to speak.

"I'll start at the beginning, a good place to make a commencement I always think. Miss Starr and I have worked together before on occasions and to our mutual advantage. Word reached me that she wished me to meet up with her for the purpose of a scheme, a big one. Having nothing of a pressing nature——"

"It'll be morning soon," Mark put in.

The Deacon sniffed and eyed Mark as if the blond giant had been a member of a jury which found against his client. "I will try to condense my story, *sir*. Nor will I go into details of Miss Starr's scheme beyond saying that it entailed gaining the confidence of a rich Virginia City business man, a hard-headed and hard-hearted cuss who was not above stooping to take an unfair advantage, and had been known not to even bother to stoop. Miss Starr handled the matter with her customary skill and this hard-headed grasper fell in love with her. Not, I hasten to add, that Miss Starr allowed anything improper to happen. She was not that kind of girl, and also, to have given in would make her seem like all the other women who fell to our pigeon's charm. I saw much of him and I can tell you towards the end he had it bad."

"Bad enough to want to kill Belle when he learned she'd fooled him?" Calamity inquired, grinning a little at the Deacon's pompous manner of speaking.

"Not as I figure him," answered Connery, "and the foibles of human nature is my hobby and profession. No, Be—the pigeon would not wish to kill Belle. You see, she outsmarted him, took him for a considerable sum of money. His feelings would be hurt badly——"

"Which could be a reason for killing," Dusty remarked.

"I know the man, Captain Fog," said the Deacon indignantly. "And while I would hardly call Cockburn a truthful man, I believe him this time. Apart from Cockburn being too scared to lie, it would fit in with what I knew of the pigeon that he sent men to take Miss Starr back to him. No doubt he would have tried to force her to marry him, and would have made a good husband had he succeeded. Alive she would have proved that nobody put anything over, dead—well, he would always know that somebody beat him at his own game and he could not bear the thought of that. No, gentlemen, I doubt if Ben—the pigeon would want Miss Starr dead."

"Anyways," Calamity put in. "This feller didn't know where to find Belle. So if he's out, where are we now?"

"Here," Dusty answered, "waiting for the Kid."

"And that's all we can do for a spell," Mark went on. "I'd say we caught up on some sleep and comes morning we'll head for town to ask questions."

Nobody objected, so after eating supper the party went

to their respective rooms for the night. In the morning the Deacon took his departure, but Dude stayed on to lend Dusty, Mark and Calamity a hand with some outstanding chores around the place. Not until evening did the two Texans and the girl find time to ride into Lubbock. None of them spoke much on their way into town, but Dusty kept glancing at the dark clouds forming in the sky.

"Looks like rain," Calamity remarked.

"You could say that," Dusty answered.

"I just did!" the girl sniffed.

"Let's go see the sheriff," Dusty said.

"Why, 'cause I saw it was going to rain afore you did?" asked Calamity.

"Because every time it rains around here, there's accidents begin to happen all over the place."

"Maybe there'll be a few more tonight," Mark put in. "It's a pity we don't know where they'll happen so we could have a few folks on hand to see they didn't."

"Yeah," Dusty drawled. "It's a real pity."

Something in the small Texan's voice brought his companion's eyes to him. Both knew Dusty well enough to figure that he had a few thoughts on the subject of where the next series of "accidents" might happen.

Sheriff Duffin sat in his office playing poker with two of his deputies when Dusty's party arrived. Scooping away the cards, the sheriff told one of his men to make some coffee, then turned his attention to his guests.

"Town's quiet now," he told them. "Been no more accidents."

"I wasn't expecting any," Dusty answered. "There's been no rain."

"Which same's just started to change," Calamity remarked, nodding towards where spots of water splashed on the window panes.

"Reckon you'll have some more accidents tonight!" Dusty said calmly.

"Why to——" a deputy asked. "Hell, yes! The others all come on rainy nights. But why——?"

"So that the rain'll wash away all tracks," Dusty explained.

"That's why they only hit on rainy nights. I've got the basic idea of the game, Bill. All the accidents are aimed at stirring the settlers up against the Indians. If there's trouble, the army will move in and restore order, then there'll be an inquiry into what started the fuss. And they'll learn that a few apparently unconnected "accidents" have been blamed on the Indians, without any proof that they were to blame. Which would satisfy those Radical Republicans and others who want to clear the settlers out of Oklahoma."

"Those Radicals tried all along to get the trail strip cleared of whites so as to cut Texas off from the beef market and prevent us getting back on our feet again after the War," Mark went on. "Only they couldn't force it through. Now that railroads are moving into Texas there won't be so many objects to giving the land back to the Indians, especially if it looks like there's going to have trouble here. Congress don't like spending money on things unless those things bring in votes come election time."

"But what do the Injuns gain by getting rid of the whites?" Duffin asked. "We allus got on well enough."

"The man behind the plan gets something," Dusty replied. "He gets power. He'll have proved his medicine, cleared the white men from Indian land. A man with that much of the Great Spirit's backing could be real big among the tribes."

Knowing Indians, none of the others needed further explanation. A war chief with a plan could only gather and retain his followers while his luck—or as they regarded it, the support of the Great Spirit's medicine—stayed with him. Should any part of his plan fail, his medicine was broken and he lost support.

"It's sure a pity we can't do us some medicine busting, Dusty," Calamity said, eyeing the small Texan hopefully.

"We might just be able to do that," Dusty answered.

"Just what's in that tricky Rio Hondo mind, Dusty?" asked Mark.

"Just a fool idea, but it might come off."

A faint smile flickered on Mark's face as he thought of other times that Dusty came up with a "fool" idea and it came off a winner.

"Going to tell us about it?" Calamity inquired.

"Sure, Calam. I reckon I'll get around to it."

"Anything you want, Cap'n," Duffin put in, "just ask for it."

"It'll take all your regular deputies," Dusty warned, "and a few more."

"I'm allus willing to do anything that'll keep the peace," the sheriff stated. "Just tell me what you aim to do and how me and the boys can help."

Given the sheriff's approval, Dusty explained his "fool" idea, a piece of strategy aimed at countering the Indian plan for clearing the white settlers from the trail strip. He tried to put himself in the planner's place, to think as the other thought, and then worked out how to defeat the plan. Using the knowledge the Kid gave him on the subject of Indian mentality, Dusty figured out the most likely next objectives at which the raiders aimed to strike. After telling Duffin and the others what he figured to happen, and why, Dusty laid out his own counter-plan. The sheriff wasted no time and soon all Duffin's deputies, augmented by a number of reliable townsmen, gathered in the office to receive orders.

Although the rain slackened during the early hours of

the night, it continued to fall and shortly after midnight increased in force. Hooves deadened by the rain and soft condition of the ground, a party of Indian horsemen came towards the town. Splitting into trios, the party separated and left their horses to advance on foot towards the darkened buildings which formed the town of Lubbock. One member of each party carried a large can which gave forth splashing noises as he walked.

The trio approaching the side door of a large building, standing slightly away from the town's limits, moved fast and silently. Then one of their number came to a halt.

"I don't like it, this business," he stated.

"Elk is a fool," jeered another. "He thinks the white man's God will not like what we do to this place."

"Elk forgets that soon the white man's God will have gone from our land," the third man answered and shook the can he carried. "Let us do our work and go."

Elk sucked in a deep breath and shoved open the door of the building. Stepping inside, the three men halted.

"Let us start the fire quickly," Elk remarked.

"Strike a——" the second man replied.

His words chopped off as a light suddenly appeared, only his friends did not cause it. A couple of lanterns, hidden under buckets until the right moment, glowed brightly on being uncovered, lighting the interior of a small church— and four armed white men who faced the Indians.

Standing at the hinges of the door, Dusty Fog thrust it shut with one hand, the other cocking his Colt as he threw down on the Indians. Elk's party, taken by surprise, left their escape just a shade too late.

"This is the place of God," Dusty told the three as they started to turn in his direction. "Let's not make a fuss inside."

Two more Colts and a brace of Winchesters gave strength

to Dusty's suggestion. Seeing they had no chance of escape, and possessing only one rifle between them—Agent Tiltman now kept the armory locked and held the key, preventing the raiders gaining access to the Springfields—the Indians surrendered.

"You called the play just right, Cap'n," enthused one of Dusty's party as he took the Indians' solitary firearm.

"Stinking redskins," another growled. "Now we'll have us a hanging."

"Mister," Dusty put in, his voice low, gentle, yet menancing as the purring snarl of a jaguar. "There's only one way you can hang these Indians—by passing me."

Quietly though Dusty spoke, his words brought to an end any desire the rest of the party might hold in the matter of hanging captives. One of the men gave a low chuckle and looked at the others.

"You've convinced us, Cap'n," he said. "Let's go see if the others have licked our catch."

"We'll wait a spell," Dusty answered. "Tie them up, and keep them quiet."

While Miss Martha Jane Canary liked the smell of horses, she preferred it out in the open, not in a barn on a rainy night. Crouched in one of the stalls, trying to make herself as comfortable as possible, she heard the man beyond the separating wall stirring restlessly. Clearing this one did not approve of any part of the business of guarding the Lubbock City livery barn.

"Huh!" he grunted in a carrying whisper. "There'll be nothing happen."

"You got anything better to do?" asked Calamity in a low, savage hiss.

"Sure I have."

"Thought you weren't married," she grinned. "For shame on you!"

Low chuckles came from the two men hidden at different points in the barn and the third crouching on the hinges side of the door on the left of the building. The owner, one of the party, always barred his main doors on the inside, but left the side door unfastened so that any traveler who wished to use his accommodation could enter. Having taken this point into consideration, Dusty ordered that one of the party prepared to close the door should the raiders come, thereby bottling off their escape. Dusty put Calamity in command of the party, which did not meet with at least one member's approval, and gave definite instructions about the treatment of any captives.

The complaining man subsided into low mutters of which Calamity only caught some *sotto voce* reference to "danged females." Under less demanding circumstances Calamity would have taken up the challenge and defended female rights to equality, or even female superiority over the male of the species. However, Calamity knew better than to allow her inclinations in that line to interfere with the correct following of Dusty's orders. So she contented herself with the thought that the complaining one was missing whatever he had to do that was better than waiting out the dark hours in the barn.

Ten minutes dragged by and Calamity had just started to wonder if maybe for once Dusty called the play wrong. Then door hinges squeaked across the room. Shooting out one hand, the girl gripped the rim of the bucket which covered a lit lantern and with the other hand shook loose the coils of her whip. She hoped that the other members of her party would remember to await her signal and not spring the trap before their prey stood well within its jaws.

Darker than the blackness of the door's outline, first one then two more shapes showed briefly and disappeared again. For almost ten seconds Calamity waited, but no more men entered. Deciding that the party consisted of but three members, she jerked the cover from her lantern.

"Now!" she yelled.

Light flooded out as the men in her party uncovered their lanterns. The livery barn owner slammed home the door, then brought up his ten gauge shotgun to cover the three startled Indians. Taken by surprise, the trio of college Indians paused far too long before thinking of escape. One of them started to raise his rifle but Calamity stepped forward. Up swung her right arm, the whip's lash flew out, wrapped around the barrel of the rifle and jerked it towards the floor.

The other two Indians froze, one letting the unopened can of kerosene he brought along fall to the ground. Moving forward, the white men disarmed the Indians. The livery barn's owner left his post and walked to where the can lay. Picking it up, he shook it, then sniffed at it. Fury gripped him as he thought of what a kerosene-induced fire would have done to his stock and property.

"You dirty red hellions!" he snarled. "I ought to shoot you down right now."

"Only you won't, Fritz," Calamity put in quietly, her whip's lash coiling up to drape over her shoulder and behind her. "Now will you?"

Angry though he might be, the barn's owner could still put two and two together and bring up an answer of four. Which meant he knew that Calamity did not intend to allow anybody to countermand Dusty Fog's orders concerning the welfare of any prisoners taken by his medicine-breaking parties.

Slowly the anger ebbed out of the owner and a grin took its place. "I won't, Calamity," he promised. "By cracky though, Cap'n Fog called it right."

"He mostly does," Calamity answered. "Hawg-tie 'em

boys. That's unless any of you object to taking orders from a gal."

Apparently nobody objected, for the tying and gagging of the Indians went by without argument. Then the party settled down with only one lamp burning to wait for further orders.

Standing behind the schoolhouse door, Mark Counter watched the three Indian raiders enter. Slowly he reached out his hand ready to close the door, blocking their escape. The first two Indians, dressed in town style clothing, continued to walk forward, but the third came to a halt. No mission-school educated Indian this one, but a bad-hat buck who in the old days would have risen to war-leader by his raiding ability and tough fight-savvy. He retained all the old-time Indian instincts, including both caution and a keen pair of ears. Either some slight sound or sensing a hostile presence alerted the buck, bringing him swinging round in Mark's direction and sending a hand reaching for a weapon.

Only Mark moved just a shade faster. Even as the Indian's revolver slid out from its holster, steel hard fingers clamped on his neck. He was lifted from the ground and pitched forward so that he smashed into his two companions, knocking them sprawling an instant before they could react to the danger. Mark kicked the door closed and he threw his captive forward and light flooded the schoolroom. All three Indians went down in a heap on the floor.

Snarling in rage, the bad-hat buck rolled free of his companions and came to his feet. Steel glinted in his hand as, having lost his revolver, he grabbed for a reserve weapon. Eight-and-a-half inches of razor sharp Green River knife blade licked around in Mark's direction as the blond giant began to move forward and block the buck's escape route.

The Indian held his knife in typical fashion, gripping the hilt so that the blade lay across his hand, allowing only slashing blows downwards or across. Electing to go down, the buck aimed a slash across at Mark's belly. Jerking himself backward into the wall, Mark avoided the slash and as the hand went by him delivered a stamping kick to its owner's leg, damn near busting the knee-cap. Following up on the kick, Mark caught the knife-arm with his left hand and brought his right around in a punch which sank into the buck's middle, jack-knifing him over.

Hard though the blow landed, there was still need for Mark to jerk the trapped arm up into the air and grip its shoulder with his other hand so as to force the buck down. Winded by the blow, hurt by the kick, that buck still fought on. Mark bent back on the wrist and thrust forward on the shoulder. A scream burst from the buck as his arm broke and the knife clattered to the floor. Jerking the man erect, Mark threw a fist which caught a red chin and dumped the buck unconscious to the floor.

"Whooee!" gasped one of Mark's party, coming forward and looking down. "Why that there's Charlie Wild-Horse. A lot of folks, red and white, 'll sleep easier knowing he's been caught."

"Likely," Mark answered, looking down at the powerful, burly frame of an Indian badly wanted for various crimes ranging from horse-stealing to rape. "Fix up those pair and let's hope that the noise didn't scare off the other bunches afore they make their moves."

Glass tinkled as a window broke in the Bold Eagle saloon, then three Indians climbed through the shattered frame.

"We take plenty fire-water with us," said one of the trio. "Charlie Wild-Horse tell us do it."

"Bar's closed Injun," answered a voice and in the sudden rush of illumination the trio found themselves covered by shotguns in the hands of Sheriff Bill Duffin and a quartet of townsmen.

The brave who suggested taking the whisky with them was made of sterner stuff than the other pair—or as a member of the Wild-Horse gang he knew his fate on being captured. Down lashed his hand, grabbing out a revolver. Duffin's shotgun bellowed and lead ripped into the buck, hurling him backwards.

"Hold your fire!" Duffin roared as his men prepared to get into the game by killing an Indian. "The other two've given up."

Although the shotgun's blast came too late to save three parties, a fourth headed for the bank, caught the warning and pulled out fast. Not one of the trio thought of riding back and warning the people who sent them out on the mission of arson, instead they fled for the safety of their own villages.

On Pilsen's ranch, Duffin's first deputy, Stalky, helped rout an attempt at fire-raising, then quieted down the settler's desire to hang two prisoners. Dude, Herb and Jack Starr drove off another bunch which visited the Starr place. In two other places attempts at creating "accidents" failed due to Dusty Fog's strategy in thinking like the other side's leader, then countering his moves.

CHAPTER FIFTEEN

I Killed You, Belle Starr!

"It happened just like you said, Cap'n, "the owner of the livery barn said after crossing from the wall rack where he had replaced the borrowed rifle after returning to the sheriff's office with his prisoners.

The rest of the men crowding into the office rumbled their agreement.

"The church, schoolhouse, livery barn, saloon; found a can of kerosene out back of the bank, even if the Injuns did get scared off," another man enthused. "How'd you know where they'd hit, Cap'n Fog?"

"Just worked out where'd be the places most likely to stir folks up greatest if they happened to burn down," Dusty explained. "You folks raised money, worked hard to build the church and school. Most of you keep horses in the livery barn, got your money in the bank; for them as don't go much on church doings, I figured losing the saloon'd rile them. Reckon some of the ranches'll be hit at too. Against the settlers and the town, Bill wouldn't be able to do much holding back when the shouts to hit the Indians started in the morning."

"What'll we do now, Cap'n?" the saloon-keeper inquired.

"Go back to bed, I reckon."

"But the In——"

"They'll keep until Bill can bring the U.S. marshals down here to make an investigation," Dusty told the men. "Only don't any of you get fool notions."

"We'll stop anybody who does," Mark promised.

"Only fool notion I've got is to get back to bed," grinned one man.

"And me," agreed another.

Soon all the townsmen had trooped off into the rain, leaving Duffin with the two Texans and Calamity. Closing the office door, Duffin turned and walked back to his desk, taking a seat.

"That handles the Injun troubles, I reckon," he said, "Only we're no closer to leaning who killed Belle."

"Tried talking to the Injuns we brought in?" asked Calamity, setting a coffeepot on the stove.

"They're not ready to answer yet," Duffin replied. "I figure to let 'em sit and stew for a spell. When they get figuring their leader's medicine done went bad on him, they'll talk. Say, I never did learn everything about the Belle affairs."

While waiting for the coffee to brew, the men and girl started to discuss the killing, kicking it around between them as peace officers often did when involved in a difficult case. As he often did while mulling over some business, Duffin began to pace the floor. Passing the rifle rack, something caught his eye and held it. One of his temporary deputies had foolishly placed a rifle back in the rack without clearing the chamber. Duffin took the offending weapon down, listening to Calamity once again bring up the matter of why the killer troubled to unload the shotgun after killing Belle. Working the lever of the rifle, Duffin ejected a bullet; it sailed across the room and landed on Dusty's foot.

Dusty glanced down at the bullet, then his eyes lifted to the rifle. Coming to his feet, Dusty slapped a hand down hard on the desk top.

"Lord, what a blind fool I was!" he said. "I had a double

barrelled gun on my mind all the time—Mark! We're taking a ride."

"Where to?" asked the blond giant.

"That Indian college."

"I'm coming along, Dusty," Calamity stated. "Let's get our fishes, it's still raining." She paused and glanced at the rack where her kepi hung with the men's hats. "That damned lid of mine doesn't hold the rain out very well."

"Got a small Stetson here you can use, Calam," Duffin answered. "You reckon you're on to something this time, Cap'n?"

"I reckon I am, Bill," Dusty agreed. "What riles me is that I never saw it in the first place."

He said no more and the others did not question him on the subject. Taking the hat Duffin offered, Calamity tried it for size, found it fitted well enough for her purpose, then donned her yellow fish. Two men also put on their waterproof clothing, then all three headed for the livery barn to collect and saddle their horses. Dusty did not mention his theory for he had no wish to raise Mark's hopes by giving a false lead. On their arrival at the Indian college, Dusty wanted Mark's mind to be open, or it might go badly for the man they rode to visit.

With the rain continuing to slash down, none of the trio said much during the ride. The river had risen, but they still managed to ford it and rode on through the unlit village. A dog growled and began to bark, but it stayed in the shelter of a cabin and made no move to chase the trio as they rode by. Once through the Agency village area, they continued to hold their horses at a fast walk and soon came in sight of the college. Again no lights showed and only a few horses stood disconsolately rump into the rain within its confines.

"Reckon you could take the other buildings, Calamity?" Dusty asked. "I don't think there'll be anybody in them."

"Take your carbine and scream if there is," Mark went on.

"Happen I take my carbine," the girl answered, "who-ever's there can do the screaming."

Sliding her carbine from the saddleboot, Calamity faded off into the darkness. The two men watched her go, then both swung their saddles. Stepping on to the porch of Ede's cabin, they halted one on each side of the door. Having done this kind of thing many times, Dusty and Mark knew the drill without needing to think. Under the shelter of the porch's roof they removed their fish, leaving clear access to their guns.

"How do we play it, Dusty?" Mark asked.

"Don't figure he's dangerous. I'll knock and we'll see what happens."

Reaching around while still standing by the wall and clear of the door, Dusty knocked loudly. Nothing happened for a few seconds, so he hammered again, even louder. Still nothing. Dusty exchanged glances with Mark, seeing the other held a Colt. Drawing his own left-hand gun, Dusty moved around to stand before the door.

"Let me take it," Mark suggested.

Before either of them could make a move at kicking in the door, they saw a light glow in the front room. Moving back to their original positions, they stood against the wall and Dusty reached out to knock again.

"All right! All right!" came Ede's voice from inside. "I'm coming."

Bare feet padded on the floor and halted by the door. Apparently Ede had set his lamp down on a table and he also appeared to have misgivings about his rashness in approaching the door.

"Who is it?" he asked.

Mark stepped around to face the door, ducked a shoulder

and lunged forward. Two hundred and ten pounds of bone and muscle struck the door. Timber cracked and the entire structure went inwards. The blond giant's charge carried him into the room, but he kept his feet. Struck by the Counter propelled door, Ede went over and he landed with a crash. An instant after Mark broke in, Dusty followed. The small Texan flung himself through the door to the left, going in low and with his Colt ready for use.

Weapons were not needed. Sat on the floor, clad in a long night-shirt, feet bare and hair tousled, Ede presented a comic rather than menacing picture but neither Texan laughed. A mixture of rage and fear etched itself on Ede's face as he stared up at his unexpected visitors.

"Wh—What do you want?" he managed to get out.

There Ede had a good point if only he knew it. Certainly Mark could not answer the question of why they came to the college and burst in on one of its staff in such a manner. Dusty alone had the answer and he did not make it in words. Crossing the room, he jerked open the cupboard's door and looked inside. Reaching in, he jerked the clothing about, then swung around to face Ede.

"All right, Ede," he growled. "Where are they?"

"Wh—Where are what?" Ede croaked.

Holstering his Colt, Mark bent down, laid hold of the man's night-shirt, hefted him to his feet and slammed him down in a chair. Then the blond giant bent forward and glared down at the terrified, cowering shape.

"Now, listen to me, *hombre*," Mark said, his voice throbbing with fury. "When Dusty asks you a question, start answering it—or I'll twist the answer out of your guts."

Ede stared first at Mark's face, then his eyes went down to the big hand which moved with fingers and thumb extended like hooks ready to sink into his flesh. Gone was Ede's assumed superiority, his condescending attitude of

"I've been to college, so I'm better than you." Only raw fear remained, stark and chilling terror as he watched that powerful hand moving closer to him.

"Those lever-action shotguns!" Dusty spat out. "Where are they?"

"Th—Three-Feathers took them with him as gifts for some Indians who're coming to his medicine meeting. I—I couldn't stop him, it was all his and her idea. I couldn't stop them!"

"You killed Belle!" Mark growled, ignoring the word which rose higher with each syllable.

Jerking his body backwards in the chair, Ede reared away from the reaching fingers. "No—No! I didn't kill her. It was Berth——"

At that, Ede's words chopped off, his mouth slumped open and his eyes bulged out of his head, staring wildly at the bedroom door through which he came. More terror than before showed on Ede's face and brought the two Texans swinging around to look in the direction he stared. Both Dusty and Mark drew their guns, but they held their fire.

Clad only in a nightgown, her hair rumpled and untidy, Bertha Ford stood at the bedroom door. In her hands she gripped a single-barrelled gun which looked, with its cocking lever, like a rifle; except that no rifle ever had such a large bore. Fury, madness almost, glowed in the woman's eyes as she glared at the three men in the center of the room.

"You swine, Ede!" she hissed. "It was all your fault. You became infatuated by her and told her enough to start her after us."

"No, Bertha!" Ede screeched. "No. I didn'——"

"You threw me over for that Southern bitch!" the woman went on, bringing the shotgun to her shoulder. "She learned all about the plan and sent for help! But I stopped her. I sent a message to her, pretending it was from you, asking her to meet you on the north road. She came and I was waiting."

"Easy, Mark!" Dusty warned as a low growl left the blond giant's throat.

Only by an effort of his will did Mark hold himself in check. While he did not shoot, he wanted to get his hands on the woman, to crush the life from her as she took it from Belle. Yet common sense told him that long before he could reach her she would squeeze the trigger and not even his giant frame was capable of standing up under the impact of a charge of buckshot.

"Bertha!" Ede screamed, starting to rise from his chair and holding out his hands in a pleading gesture. "Bertha, I never——"

"Liar!" she screamed and her finger tightened on the trigger.

Flame lashed from the shotgun's barrel and nine buckshot balls, hardly spread from their original emergence out of the barrel, ripped into Ede's chest. Such was the power of impact that Ede's body lifted from the floor, struck and shattered the chair and went down.

Bertha Ford worked on the shotgun's lever, an empty case ejected and landed on the ground. Throwing himself backwards, Dusty missed death by inches. Only the fact that the shot had not yet begun to spread saved him, for the woman jerked the gun around slightly as she triggered off another charge. Again the lever worked, but still neither Texan could bring himself to shoot at a woman.

Even as the woman worked the lever again, she stiffened, staring at the open door of the cabin. Fear wiped the madness and fury from her face and every vestige of color left her cheeks. Dusty and Mark twisted around and what they saw handed them almost as much of a shock as the one received by the woman.

A shape approached the door, coming from the blackness into the light. Although wearing a yellow-rain-slick fish, from under which showed men's pants and boots, the figure was clearly feminine. The Stetson she wore threw a shadow on her features, but something white trailed down out of its crown, hanging to the shoulders of the fish. Gripped in the shape's hands, a Winchester carbine slanted hip-high towards the inside of the cabin.

"No!" Bertha Ford gasped, staggering back the step she had taken forward on shooting Ede, "No!" I killed you, Belle Starr!"

Then she caught her balance and threw up the shotgun once more. Shocked into immobility for once in their lives, the two Texans stood by and watched the drama play out. Even though they guessed what had happened, neither could force himself to cut down Bertha Ford.

The need did not arise. Calamity dived forward, dropping to the ground and throwing up her carbine as she fell. Loud in the room came the crash of the shotgun and wood erupted in a cloud of splinters from the door about three inches above the girl's body. Then Calamity landed on her stomach and her carbine's crack came in answer to the shotgun's boom. A hole appeared in the center of the nightgown's left breast, a second springing into view an instant later as Calamity worked the carbine's lever, fed home another bullet and cut lose once again. From such close range a flat-nosed .44 bullet packed considerable shocking power. Caught by the two loads from Calamity's carbine Bertha Ford reeled backwards, dropping the shotgun and falling out of sight into the bedroom.

Silence fell on the room after the roaring of guns died away, and the draught through the open door stirred powder smoke around the space. Slowly Calamity lowered her carbine, her normally tanned face as white as the woman's had been. In falling, Calamity's Stetson came off and the white bandana she trailed down from under its crown on hearing Bertha Ford's screaming—reading the implication behind the noise even without catching the words—slipped to the floor.

Just as Calamity started to rise, her eyes went to the damage caused on the door by the shotgun's charge. From there the girl looked across the room, staring at the gun which lay where Bertha Ford dropped it.

"Th—That's a scattergun!" she gasped. "I thought it was a rifle."

"So did I the first time I saw it," Dusty admitted. "I looked into the cupboard when I came over here that day and saw three of them. But I had my mind set on double-barrelled guns and seeing the single barrel and lever threw me. I forgot about these new-fangled lever-action scatters being on sale. Now I see why Ede acted scared when I asked him questions about his owning a shotgun."

"*She* killed Belle!" Mark put in, his voice little more than a whisper.

"And now she's dead," Dusty replied. "Or is she? We never looked."

"I shot the only way I dared," Calamity stated. "It was her or m—I think I'm going to be sick!"

"Take Calam out of here, Mark," Dusty ordered. "I'll tend to things."

There proved to be little enough to do. Both Bertha Ford and Ede lay dead. After making sure he could do nothing for the woman, Dusty left the room. He wanted a responsible member of the Indian Affairs Bureau on hand as witness before starting to search the room and figured Tiltman capable of handling the matter.

For a moment Dusty stood looking down at the woman. Bending, he drew the nightgown down to cover her exposed lower regions, then he stood erect. Studying Bertha Ford's body, he marvelled at the bigotry of her kind. Even before the death of her husband, she hated Democrats in general and Southerners in particular. Finally that hatred led her to help in organizing what could have flared into a savage and bloody war; one which would have cost not only the lives of her kind, but also brought misery and death to the Indians she pretended to care for.

Turning, Dusty walked from the cabin. On the porch Calamity leaned against the rail and Mark stood at her side, a big hand resting on her shoulder. Although Calamity had fetched up pretty badly, neither of the Texans razzed her for her momentary weakness. Way Dusty and Mark saw it, anybody who came *that* close to taking a load of buckshot in the body deserved tolerance for being sick after it.

"Why'd you pull that fool game with the bandana. Calam gal?" Dusty asked, more to distract the girl's thoughts than through interest.

"I saw there was nobody about and started back. Heard her yelling and figured to throw a scare into her. Wondered what she'd do if she saw what she took for Belle's ghost coming at her. All I needed was some blonde hair, and that bandana gave it to me—— Can't we get the hell out of here, fellers?"

"I reckon we can, Calam," Mark replied.

As if some force realized that the rain would no longer be needed, it began to slacken off and die away. Outside the room, away from the acrid stink of burnt black powder and fetid stench of newly shed blood, everything smelled fresh and clean.

"Wonder where Three-Feathers is?" Dusty said.

"Ede said something about him going to a meeting," Mark replied, taking Calamity's arm and leading her from the porch. "How'd you reckon Lon's doing, Dusty?"

"Likely be doing all right," Dusty answered. "Let's go to the Agency."

And Dusty guessed right. In a cave to the north, the Ysabel Kid lay asleep, Rainey Smith's arms locked tightly about his neck and her face nestled against his shoulder.

CHAPTER SIXTEEN

Dusty's Decision

Things moved swiftly over the next two weeks. On hearing of the averted uprising, the Governor of Oklahoma Territory ordered a big investigation. Tongues loosened remarkably among the college Indians as they sought to escape punishment. Eagerly the Indians laid the blame jointly among Mrs. Ford, Ede and Three-Feathers. On his return from the hideout Blue Duck gave more information. It had been Blue Duck who first brought Belle Starr into the business. On entering the college, he found himself invited to a meeting the results of which caused him to worry about the future safety of his people. On telling Belle what he knew, the girl insisted that they gathered complete proof before laying the matter in front of the authorities. Using her considerable skill, Belle infatuated Ede and from him learned much. In doing so she either aroused Bertha Ford's suspicion, or brought the fury of the older woman's jealousy on her head. Whichever reason, Bertha Ford managed to trick Belle into riding out that fateful night and killed her. Long questioning failed to produce the Indian who delivered the message which took Belle to her death. Possibly he died in the fighting.

In the end it was decided to try to hold the affair down as much as possible. Every settler who suffered damage through prearranged accidents received compensation for his losses. Only the most guilty Indians came to trail. The killing of Bertha Ford and murder of Ede went out as it happened, except that no mention was made of their part in the proposed uprising. Instead it became known that the woman shot her lover in a fit of jealous rage and was killed by a deputy in self-defense.

At last it came to an end; or as near an end as possible. Such things are not easily forgotten. Instead of protecting the underdog and gaining him his "rights," all Bertha Ford achieved was to widen the gulf between the Indians and the settlers. It was always the same.

During the fortnight, Mark spent as little time as possible on the Starr place. Too many painful memories clung to the property now that he had lost the incentive of finding Belle's killer.

Sensing Mark's feelings on the matter, Dusty gave thought to leaving for Texas. Which brought up another matter. What should Dusty do about Freddie Woods' offer. The Kid intended to marry Rainey Smith on their return to the Rio Hondo. Could Dusty also make the step?

"Hey, Mark," Jack Starr said on the afternoon the Texans announced their departure. "You'd best pull that axe out of the chopping block. Dogs-my-cat if I can move it."

"I'll tend to it now," Mark replied.

Watched by Calamity, Dusty, the Kid and Rainey, Mark walked to where the big axe stood firmly driven into the hard wood. Gripping the handle, he gave a pull which plucked the axe from its place. Just as he was about to put the axe down, he saw three logs left from his original burst of chopping.

"Never did like to leave a job half done," he said. "Set them up, Dusty."

Around swung the axe after Dusty set up a log. The sharpened head cleaved through the wood easily—too easily for it to be solid timber. Moving forward, Dusty picked up one half of the split log. Its inside had been hollowed and a plug fitted at the end so neatly that the joint did not show. Two letters fell from the cavity and Mark dropped the axe to take them up. The first proved to be an account of Belle's investigations and shed little light that had not already come out.

"Dearest Mark" [the words sprang out at the blond giant as he opened the second letter]. "If you ever read this, I will be dead, I do not write it with any premonition of death, but merely because I must tell it to somebody, if only to a sheet of paper you will never see.

"First and foremost, Mark, I love you. I have loved you ever since our first meeting. Each subsequent meeting merely made my love grow stronger and after our night together in Santa Fe I knew I could not go on without you. The chore I rode on is my last. If you come for me, I will go anywhere you wish and will try to make you a good wife. If not, I am carrying your child and will try to raise it as you would wish.

"Do not think I let the child develop merely to force you into marriage, my darling. I only knew I must have something of yours if you fail to come for me.

"No other man has come closer to me, Mark, I saved myself for you alone.

"And now I have written my thoughts, I am tempted to destroy this letter, but I will store it in the hollow log in case I ever wish to read it again.

"I love you, Mark. Yet if we cannot marry for any reason, live your life, enjoy it to the full, you will always be in my thoughts.

"All my love,

"Belle."

Mark sank down on the chopping block, his face pale. Handing the letter to Dusty, he sat erect, looking off into the far distance and seeing nothing. After reading the letter, Dusty passed it to Calamity. Tears glinted in the red-head's eyes when she handed the sheet of paper to the Kid. While reading it, the Kid let his arm slip around Rainey's shoulders and the girl moved closer to him. Then all but Calamity drew away from Mark. Gently the girl laid her hand on his shoulder.

"She meant every word of it, Mark," Calamity told him. "Maybe life won't be so easy, but you'll go on with it. Maybe one day you'll find a nice gal almost as good as Belle. When you do, don't let memories stand in your way. Belle wouldn't want that to happen."

Coming to his feet, Mark looked down at Calamity. "I never knew you could think things like that, let alone say them, Calam gal."

"Nor did I," she admitted. "I don't reckon we'll meet again, Mark. Not the old way anyhow."

"What'll you do, gal?" he asked.

"There's a feller I know. Wants to start a freight outfit and's fool enough to want me for a wife too. Maybe I'll take him up on it one day. But until then—well, ole Dobie Killem's got a contract to handle and needs good drivers. I'm headed back to join him."

Dusty stood away from the others, thinking of the events of the past weeks and about the future. With the coming of Texas railroads his work as trail boss would be at an end. Ole Devil did not grow any younger and it was time he had some of the routine responsibility around the spread took off his hands. Maybe the time had come for Dusty to start thinking of settling down. They had been good years, eventful, exciting years since the War. Dusty knew he had done a lot of useful work in those years—but maybe the time was at hand when he must set down his roots.

Sucking in his breath, Dusty turned and walked towards his friends. Mark and the Kid guessed at his decision and approved of it—especially the Kid, with Rainey hanging on his arm.

"Mark," Dusty said. "You and Lon take the bank draft down to Uncle Devil."

"And you?" asked Mark.

"I'm going back to Mulrooney to fetch Freddie."

6A